Special Delivery

Brooke and Tess: Episode One

J.A. Armstrong

ISBN 10: 1517726115
ISBN 13: 978-1517726119

Chapter One

"I have a headache the size of Mount Everest," Brooke Campbell groaned.

"It might help if you actually slept more than three hours a night," a woman's voice responded.

Brooke sighed and looked across her office at her best friend. She had met Rachel Cantrell during her first year of residency at Boston Medical Center. Rachel had been in her final year of the program. She and Brooke connected immediately. They had similar backgrounds and shared interests that went beyond the hospital walls. Ten years later the two friends found themselves at the helm of what had been Rachel's father's practice. Brooke was grateful for Rachel as both a friend and as a colleague. At times, Rachel drove her insane with her personal brand of big sisterly advice.

"That would be nice. Too bad babies don't follow a nine to five schedule," Brooke responded.

"True. Being on call can seriously suck," Rachel confessed. "But, you don't sleep when you are home, Brooke."

Brook grumbled and swiveled nervously in her office chair. "I sleep."

"Closing your eyes on the couch, in a chair, with the television blaring for a few hours does not constitute sleep. You're a doctor for God's sake. What would you advise a patient?"

"That depends," Brooke replied.

"Really?"

"Yes. If they are nine months pregnant and pending the pop, I might just advise that exact remedy."

Rachel rolled her eyes. "You are impossible."

"And, you are a nag."

"Brooke, you seriously cannot keep up this pace. When was the last time you took a real vacation? And, before you say anything, I mean to relax, not to climb some mountain or dive some barrier reef," Rachel inquired knowingly.

"Barrier Reef? Exaggerate much?" Brooke asked. "I took a vacation in February."

"To go zip lining in the rainforest!"

"What?" Brooke threw her hands up. "It was relaxing."

"Come on, you could go visit your mom," Rachel suggested. "Take a week off."

Brooke shook her head and laughed. "You are relentless. I'm okay, Rach. I have the weekend off."

"Good, so don't agree to cover anyone…"

"I got it," Brooke held up her hands in surrender.

Rachel nodded at her best friend. Brooke was the definition of a workaholic. It had always been that way. Even after many years of friendship, she couldn't pinpoint what drove Brooke to work herself to exhaustion. Some of it she suspected had to do with Brooke's upbringing. They had grown up in households where their parents were constantly on the go. Rachel's father was an OB/GYN. Brooke's parents were both surgeons, although her mother had moved to teaching after her parents divorced when she was twelve. The two women shared a fascination with medicine, much of it as a result of their fathers' passions.

Rachel had always been able to maintain balance in her life. Brooke seemed to struggle in that endeavor. For years, Rachel assumed that Brooke's frantic pace would slow once she had managed to enter a stable private practice. That still had not come to pass. In fact, after Rachel married, Brooke's life seemed to become even more harried. She dated from time to time, but she never settled in with any one person for long. She went on outings with friends, but those were nearly always adventure based, kayaking, hiking, diving, or some insane endeavor like skydiving. The only time Rachel ever saw Brooke take a breath was when Brooke spent a day at Rachel's. Even then, she insisted on taking over the grill or cleaning up after a meal. And, Brooke always stepped in for active Auntie duty, as she called it. Rachel and her husband, Mike were assured that Brooke would have their two-year-old son, Eli wrapped around her legs, her hips, or her head for the duration of her visit. Brooke insisted that she was happy with her life the way it was. Rachel wanted to throttle her and drive home the point that being used to your life a certain way did not equate to happiness.

"You're off this weekend. Why don't you come over for a cookout on Sunday?" Rachel suggested.

Brooke smiled. She had not had much of an opportunity to spend time with her best friend outside of the office in weeks. They had been keeping almost entirely opposite schedules to accommodate the vacation time of the other three doctors who shared their practice. "What are you cooking?" Brooke teased. "Should I prescribe the anti-nausea medicine now?"

"Cute, Dr. Campbell. Just be there by noon. If you're lucky, I will let Mike do the grilling," Rachel responded as she made her way out of Brooke's office.

"All right. I'll be there by one," Brooke said.

"Noon, Doc. Noon."

Brooke laughed as she watched Rachel exit. She loathed to admit it, but the thought of spending a day with Rachel's family gave her something to look forward to. She returned her focus to the computer screen in front of her. "Maybe I should bring something nice and noisy for Eli," she chuckled. "Paybacks, Dr. Cantrell. Paybacks."

"Good God, will this day never end?" Tess Sinclair mumbled. She hopped out of the driver's seat of her truck and finagled her way into the back to grab the packages for her next delivery. A small smile touched her lips when she saw the box marked for Dr. Brooke Campbell. "I wonder if the good doctor will make an appearance today," she giggled. "Good Lord! She must be keeping Amazon in business," Tess laughed. She shook her head and made her way to the back of the truck for a hand cart. She rolled up the back door, loaded the six boxes on the cart and started for the building a few yards away.

Salem Women's Health and Wellness was one of the last stops on Tess's daily route. Tess enjoyed the banter and the casual conversation that the staff always engaged in with her. It amazed her that even after seeing people repeatedly, day after day after day, more often than not, she was fortunate if she managed to get a meaningful "hello" out of people. This stop was one of three that was unique in that regard. And, there was an added benefit. Occasionally, Tess managed to catch a glimpse of a certain doctor who had captured her imagination. It had taken her nearly a month to discern who the attractive brunette was. Brooke Campbell could have been a model, or perhaps even a movie star, at least that was Tess's opinion. She noticed that the staff seemed to brighten when the doctor entered the front office.

Brooke Campbell was tall and athletic. Tess estimated she had to be close to six feet tall. She sometimes wondered if the doctor had ever considered a life in basketball. Brooke always wore her jet black hair pulled back in a ponytail. When she drew closer, Tess had noticed the streaks of natural red highlights that ran through her locks. But, it was Brooke's eyes that Tess found particularly alluring. They were crystalline blue. It gave the doctor's appearance an appealing contrast. A little crush on a beautiful woman was harmless. After all, Dr. Brooke Campbell was likely straight and more likely attached. That was perfectly fine with Tess. Romantic attachments were not a part of any appointment calendar she was keeping these days. She stopped in front of the door to the small brick building and smiled. "Well, a little diversion wouldn't hurt," she chuckled.

Brooke walked her patient to the front desk. "Soon, Maddie."

"Soon?" the woman asked. She looked down at her belly and chuckled. "Did he tell you that or are you just trying to make me feel better?" she asked Brooke.

Brooke offered her patient a lopsided grin. She had delivered the first two of Maddie Stedman's children. Kyle, was her third and officially due in a week and a half. Maddie was miserable. Brooke had learned early on never to share her predictions about when a baby would make his or her appearance. She had a sixth sense about those things at times. She and Rachel often placed friendly bets on who would be in the delivery room and when. Brooke's estimations were almost always accurate. Rachel had accused her best friend more than once of practicing voodoo on the side.

"I never betray a confidence," Brooke answered. "Doctor/patient confidentiality and all."

Maddie shook her head. "Well, I hope you are right. I would like to sleep for more than an hour at a time."

Brooke nodded. "I will see you next Tuesday unless I see you before that," she said with a wink. She turned her attention to the woman behind the reception desk. "Janine? Did Tess come yet?" she asked as she leaned over the counter to look for any evidence of the delivery driver's presence.

"Not yet," Janine giggled. "What are you expecting that is so dire? You've asked four times in the last two hours. Tess never comes before three."

Brooke huffed just as the front door opened and Tess walked through dragging the hand truck behind her. Brooke sprinted across the small office and held the door open for her. Tess jumped slightly at the closeness of the beautiful doctor. "Thanks," Tess said in surprise.

"Quite the load," Janine commented from the desk. "Is that all for her?" she pointed to Brooke. "What is it now? Scuba gear?" Brooke always had her personal purchases delivered to the office. Last year, she had discovered rock climbing. The year before that Brooke had taken up snorkeling. She was an avid hiker, camper, and cyclist. Brooke loved adventure. Janine could only imagine what the precocious doctor had taken an interest in now.

Brooke snarled playfully at the receptionist. Janine laughed at the doctor's expression. "Don't you have patients to call? Appointments to book?" Brooke asked.

"No," Janine said. "I block three to four for personal torture of my boss."

"Good. Go find Rachel and torment her while I help Tess with these," Brooke suggested.

"What are you up to?" Janine asked suspiciously. Brooke shrugged and turned back to Tess. "Would you mind dropping them in my office?"

"Not at all," Tess replied, trying to swallow the slight lump in her throat. Dr. Campbell was always friendly, but she was normally on the run. A quick hello or a wave was the extent of most interactions Tess had with the doctor.

"Thanks," Brooke said. She led Tess through a door into a small hallway and stopped. "Hold on," she whispered.

Brooke looked both ways and then beckoned Tess to follow her across the hall into her office. As soon as Tess walked through the door, Brooke closed and locked it.

Tess looked across the room at the approaching doctor curiously. "I'm almost afraid to ask," she admitted.

Brooke smiled and lifted the boxes off of the hand truck and into a small closet behind her desk. "I don't want Rachel to see," she explained. "It's a surprise." Tess nodded and handed Brooke a pad to sign for her packages. "Thanks again, Tess. I hope this little diversion doesn't put you behind," Brooke said sincerely.

"No worries," Tess assured her. "You are my last stop." Brooke opened the office door and led Tess back to the front desk. "Good luck with your surprise," Tess said. "I'll probably see you tomorrow, Janine."

"Oh, I would count on it," Janine laughed with a wave to Tess. "So?" She turned back to Brooke.

"What?"

"Don't you what me, Dr. Campbell. What are you up to?" Janine asked.

"Curiosity killed the cat, Janine."

"I have a dog," Janine deadpanned.

"We can fix that," Brooke responded before walking away.

"Oh boy," Janine mumbled. "She is definitely up to no good."

"Davey! Stop harassing your sister," Tess scolded her son.

"She started it!" Davey argued.

Tess rolled her eyes. She adored her children, but they could drive her insane at times. Twins. After eight years, Tess could still not fathom how she ended up with twins. David and Danielle were the light of Tess Sinclair's life. The unexpected light. Tess was just finishing her junior year of college when she discovered that she was pregnant. To her surprise, her Catholic parents had gently suggested that she terminate the pregnancy and finish school. Tess would not hear of it. She had hoped that her boyfriend would share her view. He did not. Daniel Medina had been Tess's boyfriend since junior high school. Tess never imagined that her longtime sweetheart would skip out on her and their children. He did. He had agreed with her parents' assessment. Tess was heartbroken. It had not occurred to her once to terminate her pregnancy. Regardless of struggles, upheavals, and the occasional mind-numbing frustration and chaos her children could create, Tess had never regretted her decision.

"Mom," Dani complained. "He's doing it again!"

"Would you two just be quiet for a few minutes? Go sit down while I get the pizza. Please," Tess implored the pair.

Dani pushed her brother toward a table in the corner. Davey twirled back to push his sister and was abruptly stopped by an immovable object. "Uh…sorry," he said sheepishly.

Tess spun on her heels and found herself staring at a familiar figure. She followed Brooke's eyes to the ground where a large pizza box had fallen open decorating the floor with pepperoni slices. "Oh, no," Tess covered her mouth with her hands.

Brooke looked up at that moment and met Tess's gaze. She pointed to Davey. "Yours?" she asked.

Tess nodded and pointed to the pizza on the floor. "Yours?" she cringed. Brooke raised her eyebrow and nodded. Tess groaned and then scolded Davey with an unappreciative gaze.

"Sorry, Mom," he said.

Brooke noted the tension in Tess's face and laughed. "It's not the worst casualty I have ever seen," she said lightly.

Tess shook her head. "I am sorry, Dr. Campbell." Tess reached over and grabbed a handful of napkins off the counter and set about the task of cleaning up the pizza on the floor.

"Brooke."

"What?" Tess looked back at the doctor who was now squatting beside her, scooping a sloppy mass of cheese into her open pizza box.

"Well, after such an intimate collision with my dinner, I think we could graduate to first names, don't you?" Brooke joked.

"Let me buy you another pizza," Tess offered.

Brooke looked at the two children who had taken up residence behind their mother and smiled. "Tell me that is not double trouble," Brooke chuckled.

Tess sighed but smiled genuinely. "Triple trouble," she said with the raise of her brow. "They don't tell you that trouble is the triplet with twins."

"That was a mouthful," Brooke commented in amusement.

"Come on, let me buy you a pizza," Tess repeated.

"Not necessary," Brooke said.

"You cannot eat *that,*" Tess scrunched her face is disapproval.

"What do you mean? I am a doctor, you know. I am sure I can repair the damage."

Tess folded her arms across her chest. "Aren't you an OB? That would take a trauma surgeon and an excellent one at that," Tess replied seriously.

Brooke frowned. "I know a good one," she said. "But, he is in California."

Tess shook her head. "Well, if you won't let me replace that mess, can I at least convince you to share ours?" The words were out before Tess could stop them. *Oh, God. She's going to think I am asking her out. Oh, God. Could this get any worse? Just kill me. Please? Strike me down where I stand.* Brooke contemplated the nervous expression on Tess's face silently. She was surprised when the young boy spoke.

"We got pepperoni too," he said innocently.

Brooke looked at him thoughtfully. "Well, in that case, how can I say no?" Tess grinned uncomfortably. "You sure that you have enough?" Brooke asked. She looked back at the twins. "Triple trouble here are willing to donate a piece of their pie to my cause?" Both kids nodded.

"We were going to head home, but we can get a table here," Tess said.

"I don't want you to change your plans on my account."

"You can come over," Dani piped up. "Mom never has friends over. Not really. Not since Jackie."

Tess blushed. "Sorry," she whispered. "Don't put Dr. Campbell on the spot," she said.

Brooke couldn't help but smile. She had always liked Tess. Tess was upbeat and engaging. Brooke often heard Janine laughing when Tess made her deliveries. She had never engaged in any meaningful conversation with the courier. And, she was surprised to see that Tess had two children. She placed the pair of brunettes at about eight or nine years old. Tess didn't appear to be much over thirty if that. Brooke was curious. "I am hungry. I don't need to charter a plane or anything to get there, do I?" she asked the kids.

"No!" Davey laughed. "We walked."

Brooke looked back at Tess for her approval. "It's just around the block," Tess explained. "You are welcome to join us, but if…"

"Lead on," Brooke said. Tess stared at her blankly in disbelief.

"Dr. Campbell," a man's voice broke through their awkward silence. "Let me get you something else. Jeremy!" he called. "Clean this up!"

"Relax, Sal," Brooke put a hand on the man's shoulder. "I should look down when I walk," she winked at Davey.

"We will get you a new one right away," Sal promised.

Tess felt disappointment sweep over her. Brooke smiled at the restaurant owner. "No need, I already have an offer for dinner."

"I am happy to replace it," Sal said again. Brooke frequented the small restaurant. She and Rachel often had lunch there and Brooke stopped at least twice a week to pick up dinner on her way home. Sal had become a friend over the years.

"How about we reserve that for another time?" she suggested. "I might need it one day," she winked.

"Whatever you say, Doc," Sal laughed.

Brooke turned back to Tess. "Offer still good?" she asked. Tess nodded dumbly. "Well, lead on. I'm starving."

Chapter Two

Brooke followed with Tess behind the two kids as they walked around the block. She reached over and took the pizza box from Tess's hands. "You don't have to carry that," Tess said.

"You paid. Seems like the least I can do is carry the goods."

"Um. You paid too. Only to have my son feed the floor with your dinner," Tess reminded the doctor.

"Eh, it gives Sal an excuse to finally clean that floor," Brooke said. She looked ahead and saw Davey chase Dani up the porch stairs of a small Cape Cod home. "Yours?" she gestured to the house. Tess nodded. "Cute," Brooke complimented.

Tess stepped up behind the kids and unlocked the door. Brooke took the cue and stepped inside. She looked around the small living room and smiled. The walls were painted a sky blue and were adorned with several paintings of seascapes. A soft beige couch sat in the middle of the room facing a stone set fireplace. Brooke noted that there was no television in the room and was surprised that other than the two portraits that sat on the mantle, there was no evidence of children in the space.

Tess handed Dani the pizza box. "Take this to the kitchen table. Carefully, please," Tess instructed. "Get washed up," she said before stepping up beside Brooke. "It's not really much. I know," Tess said softly.

Brooke was lost in her visual exploration of the room. It was stunning. The room could easily have been the common area of a quaint bed and breakfast on Cape Cod. "Did you decorate it yourself?" she asked.

"Yeah. Amazing what you can do with a few dollars. I wish I could afford some professional artwork, but I tried."

Brooke turned and looked at Tess in awe. "Are you telling me that you painted those?"

"Yeah. I know, not really..."

"They're amazing," Brooke said earnestly.

Tess wrinkled her nose. "Are we looking at the same pictures?"

Brooke moved to stand in front of one of the paintings. It depicted a rocky seashore with a dilapidated dock extending out on the right-hand side. The sun appeared to be just setting. Tess had painted the sky in pink and purple tones that reflected in the water. "Do you sell them?"

"Sell them?" Tess asked in confusion.

"Your paintings," Brooke clarified.

Tess chuckled. "No."

"You should."

"Mom!" Davey called.

"Sounds like your troops are hungry," Brooke said.

"They are always hungry," Tess replied. "Come on, or we'll be licking the crumbs from the box."

"I swear, I have never done that," Brooke crossed her heart.

Tess looked at her and giggled slightly. *Just who are you, Dr. Brooke Campbell?*

The foursome had been sitting around the table for nearly an hour and Brooke noticed that Tess had not taken one slice of pizza for herself. "Not hungry?" she asked the woman seated beside her.

"She's weird," Davey say with a mouthful. "She hates pizza."

"I am not weird," Tess defended herself. "I don't hate pizza. I hate pepperoni. And, don't talk with your mouth full," she added.

"You hate pepperoni? No one hates pepperoni," Brooke said assuredly. Davey and Dani both laughed.

"Slimy meat and I are not friends," Tess replied. Brooke's coy smile caught Tess slightly off guard.

"Yeah, Jackie hated it too. Nothing on her pizza. She was a pizza purist," Davey said innocently.

"Jackie?" Brooke asked curiously.

"Mom's ex-girlfriend," Dani said. Tess choked on the soda in her mouth. Brooke tried not to laugh.

"Everyone has at least one of those," Brooke shrugged. Tess's eyes flew open. "But, you should know to be suspicious of any woman who claims to be a pizza purist. And, really? Who doesn't like pepperoni? Do you have any other strange aversions?" Brooke asked. Tess choked again and coughed. "You okay there?" Brooke asked lightly. Tess nodded. Brooke turned her attention back to the kids. "So, now that I know your mom's issues. What about you two? I know you like pizza with pepperoni, so we are on the same page there. How about school? Like it or are you two purists?" Brooke asked seriously.

Dani giggled. "He likes gym and recess," she said, pointing to her brother.

Davey made a face at his sister. "So?"

"What about you, Dani?" Brooke asked with genuine interest.

"I like science."

"She's weird too," Davey pointed at his sister.

"Am not!" Dani snapped back.

"Science is cool. I always liked science," Brooke said. "I liked recess too," she winked at Davey.

"You did?" Dani asked in surprise.

"Yep."

"Dr. Campbell *is* a doctor," Tess reminded her children with a smile.

"You're a real doctor?" Dani asked wide eyed.

"That's what they say," Brooke responded.

"Cool. Do you see blood and guts?" Davey asked excitedly.

Tess rolled her eyes. Brooke laughed. "Sometimes," Brooke said. "Mostly, I see babies."

"Babies?" Davey wrinkled his nose. "That's boring."

Tess chuckled as she moved to pick up their plates. Brooke started to stand and Tess grabbed her hand gently to stop her. "No, you are a guest."

Brooke managed a half-hearted smile. It was in her nature to move and to help. The last thing she wanted to do was make Tess uncomfortable. The kids had spilled more than their fair share of beans about their mother to Tess's horror. Brooke had enjoyed the hour long dinner conversation. Davey and Dani were like a young Abbott and Costello. She could see the adventurous twinkle in both pairs of eyes and she could only begin to imagine the kind of trouble that caused. And, she found Tess's innocent blushing amusing and endearing.

"Mom was almost a doctor," Dani told Brooke. Tess dropped a plate in the sink at the words. She didn't often speak about her original life plans, not with anyone. She didn't see the point. Tess had no regrets about her decision to put her children first. There were times, if she were to be honest, that she wondered what life would have been like had her life taken the path she once envisioned.

Brooke looked over at Tess, who just shrugged. "Not really," Tess said softly. "I didn't even finish my bachelor's," she admitted. "And, that was a long time ago," she said.

"Grandma says you still could," Davey chimed.

"Grandma says a lot of things," Tess reminded her son. "Now, come on. You two have tormented Dr. Campbell enough, and I know you both have homework, so skip to it."

"Aww…we were just starting to talk about guts," Davey complained.

Brooke snickered. "I should probably get going," she said.

Tess forced a smile. It had never occurred to her that the object of her innocent crush would end up sitting at her kitchen table. In the short time that they had shared, Tess had grown more curious about the doctor. She didn't have many close friends. Most of her friends were still single, the few that were married either had yet to start families or they were chasing infants and toddlers. It was refreshing to have another adult at the table. "I'll walk you out," Tess said.

Brooke nodded. "You two behave," Brooke teased the twins.

"See ya, Dr. Campbell," Dani said.

"You can call me Brooke. Dr. Campbell makes me feel old."

Davey and Dani laughed. "Old people can be cool," Davey said as he ran into the other room. Tess laughed at the look of sheer horror on Brooke's face as they headed for the front door.

"Was that a compliment?" Brooke wondered aloud.

Tess shook her head. "From Davey? That was the ultimate in flattery," she promised.

"Oh, God. I am old," Brooke groaned. Tess snickered. "Listen, thanks for dinner."

"Thanks for putting up with us," Tess said. "I'm sure there is much more interesting company you could have shared a pizza with."

Brooke detected a hint of sadness in Tess's voice. She seldom shared dinner with anyone except her dog, Murphy. "Well, don't get me wrong, I love Murphy's company, but his conversation can be a bit one-sided."

"Murphy?"

"My lab," Brooke explained. Tess nodded. "I had a good time."

"Me too," Tess admitted.

"See you tomorrow?"

"In uniform," Tess said.

"Night, Tess."

"Goodnight, Dr..." Brooke's eyebrow shot up into her hairline. "Brooke," Tess said.

Brooke smiled and offered her new friend a slight wave. Tess closed the door slowly and watched as Brooke headed back down the sidewalk. Brooke was not what she had imagined. She wasn't certain what she had imagined or maybe she was. She expected to be intimidated by the doctor. There were times that Tess admittedly felt embarrassed by her lack of formal education. Brooke seemed unfazed by all of it. Maybe, just maybe, Tess had found someone she could cultivate a friendship with.

As she watched Brooke disappear around the corner, she sighed. There was no way to deny that she was attracted to the doctor. Brooke was gorgeous, intelligent, and quite charming. Dating simply was not on Tess's agenda. It was too complicated. She had spent two years with Jackie. She let her children grow attached to the woman. It had ended in disaster. Jackie had left her in a financial mess and that was not the worst of it. She had left Tess abruptly and without any thought of how it would affect Dani and Davey. The twins were only five when Jackie left. They had considered Jackie a parent. They trusted her. They loved her. Tess could deal with the betrayal. She recovered quickly. The long nights of tears from her children were a different story. For months, Davey would cry himself to sleep. He could not understand why Jackie didn't call or even say goodbye. Tess swore she would never put her children through that kind of pain again. She collapsed against the front door. It was only a dinner, somehow it conjured reality for Tess. The reality was that she was lonely. *It was just a dinner.*

Brooke peeked around the corner when she heard a familiar voice. She smiled when she saw Tess laughing with Janine.

"What are you doing?" Rachel laughed from behind her best friend.

"Me? Nothing," Brooke responded innocently.

"Uh-huh. You are still coming Sunday?" Rachel asked.

"One o'clock. I'll be there."

"Noon, Doc. Noon," Rachel smacked Brooke lightly.

Brooke stepped out into the front office and smiled at Tess. "Hey," she greeted the courier. Tess smiled.

Janine regarded the interaction curiously. "You looking for something?" she asked Brooke.

"No. Why?" Brooke asked. Tess looked at her feet.

"You usually scurry out here like a kid on Christmas that thinks Tess is Santa Claus with your packages," Janine commented.

"I do not," Brooke said. Tess smirked. "What?" she looked at Tess. "I do not scurry," Brooke said.

"Of course not," Tess agreed.

"I just was curious if I had any messages," Brooke said to Janine.

Janine looked at Brooke as if she had hit her head. "If you had messages, I would have let you know."

"I was consulting with Dr. Shaw in her office," Brooke offered a weak explanation.

"Uh-huh. Well, nope. No messages. No one is in labor—yet. And, might I remind you that as of ten minutes ago you are not the one on call."

"Thank you, Mom," Brooke said sarcastically. "Rachel has you trained."

"Too bad she hasn't succeeded with you all these years," Janine replied.

"Oh, you are a comedian. No wonder my patients are always smiling," Brooke said.

"Well, have a nice weekend," Tess said.

"You too," Janine said. "Any big plans?"

"Not a one," Tess replied. She looked at Brooke and smiled. Brooke smiled back and excused herself.

Janine rolled her eyes. "I swear she is like a big kid," Janine laughed. "Hard to believe sometimes she is the most sought after doctor here."

Tess tipped her head in curiosity. "Really?"

"Yeah. She's a rare breed. She and Dr. Cantrell both. But, Brooke? People talk. Most people think she should have been a surgeon. She's saved more than a few pregnancies and babies in her young career. That's why she ends up on call or being called when she's not on call so often. She's easy going, but she's also amazing under pressure."

Tess smiled. That was not difficult for her to believe. "Well, if I ever decide to have twins again, I will know who to call," she said.

"Good choice," Janine replied. "See you Monday."

"I certainly hope so," Tess said with a wave goodbye.

"A drum set, Brooke?" Rachel shook her head. "He's two!"

Brooke watched her honorary nephew run across the living room to where his father was playing with the junior drum set she had purchased. "What? Prodigies start young, Rach."

Rachel rolled her eyes. Mike seemed to delight in the drum set even more than Eli. "What happens when my lawyer husband wants to become a rock star? I am blaming you!" Rachel warned her best friend.

"Hey, rock stars make good money," Brooke argued.

"He loves it!" Mike called over. He had lifted Eli onto his lap. Eli was doing his best to hit the drums with the stick in his hands and screeching with delight each time he made contact.

"That's great," Rachel said with mock enthusiasm. She turned back to Brooke. "You couldn't have chosen something a bit, I don't know, quieter?"

"What would you have preferred? I give a two-year-old a scalpel?"

"Funny. What about crayons?" Rachel responded.

"Do you like your white walls?" Brooke asked.

Rachel groaned. "You are going to be babysitting—a lot."

Brooke shrugged. "I never mind hanging with the little man."

"You know, you could have your own little man to hang out with," Rachel interjected.

"I gave up little men the same time I gave up big men. That was in about the tenth grade."

"Ha-ha. You know exactly what I am talking about. What about that nice teacher you went out with a while back?" Rachel asked.

"Carmen?"

"Yeah, her. She seemed nice. She was really into you," Rachel smirked.

Brooke groaned. "Too clingy. I need my space."

"You need your own damn galaxy," Rachel replied. "You love kids. You don't have to have a partner you know. It is 2015."

"Oh, no. No way. I am not doing that single mom thing."

"Your mom was a single mom," Rachel reminded her. "For most of your life."

"Yes, and it super sucked for her. She gave up everything. Like Tess. No way. I am too selfish for that."

Rachel set down the beer she was drinking. "Like Tess? Who is Tess?"

"You know—Tess," Brooke said. Rachel lifted her hands in confusion. "Tess! Geez, Rach, you see her practically every day when she comes into the office."

"Tess as in the driver that delivers the goodies you are constantly buying online? That Tess?" Rachel asked for clarification.

"Do you see a lot of other Tesses in the office daily?"

"Tess has kids?"

"Two," Brooke answered. She laughed when Eli hit a cymbal and he startled himself.

"Huh. Did Janine tell you that?" Rachel wondered.

"Tell me what?"

"Hello! That Tess has kids!" Rachel said in exasperation.

"Oh. No. I met them Thursday," Brooke said.

"You met them? What do you mean you met them? She brought them to work?" Brooke was focused on Eli and Mike at the drum set. "Hello?" Rachel waved a hand in front of Brooke's face.

"What?"

"I asked if she brought her kids with her to work or something."

"Who?" Brooke asked.

"Tess!"

"Oh. No. We had pizza."

"When did you have pizza? Wait. What do you mean you had pizza?"

Brooke shrugged. "That shouldn't be a hard concept, even for you," she teased her friend. "It comes in a box, sliced. You open the box and eat it."

Rachel narrowed her gaze menacingly. "Yes, I know. Who did you eat this pizza with?"

"I told you. I had pizza with Tess and her kids."

"Wait. You asked Tess out and she brought her kids? Is that what you are telling me?" Rachel asked.

"What? No."

"Explain yourself," Rachel demanded.

"God, you would think I announced a marriage or something. It was just pizza."

"Pizza does not surprise me. You eat pizza at least four times a week. Pizza with a woman and her children? That surprises me," Rachel said.

"I bumped into them at Sal's. Actually, Davey bumped into me," Brooke explained.

"Davey?"

"Tess's son."

"Uh-huh. And?"

"And?" Brooke shrugged. "My pizza was a casualty of said bumping. Tess offered to buy me a new one. I declined. Tess offered to share their pizza. I accepted."

"Huh," Rachel mused quietly. Brooke kept her attention squarely on Eli at the drum set. He was banging and clanging in no particular order or rhythm, but he was apparently pleased with the noise he was producing. That delighted Brooke. "So? What's she like?" Rachel asked as she lifted her beer again.

"Who?" Brooke asked.

"Tess, you idiot!"

Brooke chuckled. "Why are you so interested in Tess?" she asked playfully.

"The question is, are you?" Rachel replied.

"Am I what?"

"Interested in Tess!" Rachel nearly yelled to be heard over the banging in the background.

"She is interesting," Brooke admitted.

"Yeah? So, are you interested in her?"

"You mean like romantically?" Brooke raised her voice to be heard.

"I mean like at all," Rachel said.

Brooke shrugged. *Am I?* "I like her," she admitted.

"You like her or you *like* her?"

"Are we in seventh grade," Brooke laughed. "She's a nice person. I like her."

"Um-hum. She's straight, huh?" Rachel guessed.

"What?"

"Tess. She's straight. Two kids, looking for a good husb..."

Brooke burst out laughing. Rachel's' assumption conjured an image of Tess's face when her kids innocently had outed her at dinner. "Two kids, yes. Straight? Not so much."

"Really? She told you or is it that gaydar thing?"

"Gaydar thing?" Brooke snickered. "No, Dani sort of let it slip."

"Dani?" Rachel inquired.

"Tess's daughter."

"Oh. Whoops," Rachel chuckled. "So? Are you?"

"What?"

"Come on, Brooke! Tess is cute."

Brooke smiled unconsciously. *Yes, she is cute. Especially when she is embarrassed.* "I guess she is."

"So, you're not interested in her?"

"Will you stop already? Are you taking bribes from Match.com or something?" Brooke wondered in amusement.

"No. I just would like to see you happy."

"I am happy."

"Okay, I would like to see you happier," Rachel corrected herself. "And, not so alone."

"Last I looked, I was not alone," Brooke chided.

"You know what I mean."

"Rach, I love you. I do. Just let it go, okay?" Brooke implored her friend just as Eli came running full tilt toward her.

He held out his arms and Brooke swooped him up onto her knee, an enormous smile lighting her face as he reached out for her.

Rachel watched her best friend with her son. She shook her head slightly. She knew Brooke as well, if not better than anyone, except perhaps Brooke's mother. There was no doubt in Rachel's mind that Brooke was lonely much of the time. She had never been able to figure out what held her best friend back from attachments, particularly romantic ones. Brooke had dated some remarkable women over the years. More than a few had expressed an interest in furthering their relationship. As soon as things looked like they were progressing, Brooke inevitably pulled back. It left Rachel wondering if Brooke simply had not met the right woman or if she feared commitment for some reason. If it was the latter, Brooke had never shared the reason why with Rachel. *Oh, Brooke. What is it that you are not telling me?*

"Do you want to give him his bath? I know you like to play with those rubber duckies," Rachel said.

Brooke stood and lifted Eli onto her hip. "Do you want to play duckies?" she asked the toddler.

"Fuckies!" he yelled. Brooke nearly choked she laughed so hard.

Rachel shook her head and sighed. "He can't say D's too well," she explained. "Duh, Eli. Duh.. Duuuckies. D-uckies."

"Fuckies! Book, fuckie tubby!"

Brooke laughed and arched her brow at Rachel. "Just what are you teaching my nephew," she whispered. "Come on, Eli. Auntie Brooke will sing the alphabet to you." Rachel watched her best friend disappear up the stairs.

"What were you too gossiping about?" Mike asked as he took a seat beside his wife.

"Nothing. I just don't understand her sometimes. I worry about her."

"Brooke? Why? What's wrong with Brooke?"

"Nothing she is telling me," Rachel answered quietly.

"Rach, she's got her own life to live," Mike said gently.

"I know. I just wish she would actually give herself a chance to live it."

Mike sighed. "You never know what's in store," he said with a kiss on his wife's cheek. "And anyway, I am kind of glad she hasn't settled down with anyone yet."

"What? Why would you say that?"

"Free babysitting, honey."

Rachel chuckled. "Yeah, well. I hope she does. And, not just for her sake."

"What does that mean?"

"I guarantee Eli will get fewer noise makers if she ever does."

Mike laughed. "See, you do have a hidden agenda."

"Nope. Nothing hidden about it," Rachel said bluntly. *One day, Brooke. One day, there will be paybacks. I feel it.*

Chapter Three

It had been a long week for Brooke and the week was about to get even longer. She had stepped in to cover Regina Shaw earlier in the week. Dr. Shaw had been a part of their practice for the last year. She was also pregnant with her first child and was suffering a bout of severe all day long morning sickness. Brooke had taken double appointments and come into the office on her day off so that Regina could stay home and rest. Now, it was Friday and Brooke was officially the primary doctor on call for emergencies, labor, and delivery. There were no less than four patients that she expected might find themselves in the delivery room over the weekend. And, there were also some high-risk patients that both she and Rachel were concerned about. She was sitting at her desk reviewing notes when Rachel's head popped into the doorway.

"Got a minute?" Rachel asked.

"Yeah, of course. I was just looking at the notes you wrote in Daisy Menendez's file."

"That's what I wanted to talk to you about," Rachel said.

Brooke set down the file and regarded her best friend thoughtfully. Rachel was a gifted doctor. She was also an empathetic person. One of the things that always bonded Brooke and Rachel was their genuine concern and compassion for the people they treated and cared for. Most of the time, their work ended in a cause for celebration. They both prided themselves on that. Occasionally, an outcome was less than desirable. Once in a great while, both were faced with tragedy. The death of an infant at birth, the crisis of a mother in labor that could not be foreseen, or the termination of a long-awaited pregnancy, these were the moments that could shake both Rachel and Brooke to their core. The best any doctor could do was to be diligent, to be attentive, and to make every attempt to anticipate and prepare for the unthinkable.

Daisy Menendez had been Rachel's patient for six years. She had lost two pregnancies and struggled to become pregnant a third time. Her biological clock was ticking. Rachel was an expert in fertility treatment. People sought her counsel and her skill in conceiving. Brooke was an expert in women's health and in gynecological surgery. Rachel had suggested more than once that Brooke should consider leaving the practice and pursuing surgery as her discipline. Brooke declined. She enjoyed surgery when the need arose. At the same time, she prayed that the need to hold a scalpel would be kept to a minimum.

"You're worried. More than your notes indicate," Brooke surmised.

Rachel sighed. "I am. She has hypertension and GDM, Brooke."

"I know. I read your notes. You saw her yesterday?"

"Yeah."

"How did she seem? And, I don't mean her vitals or her blood sugar. I mean, how did she *seem*?"

"Anxious."

Brooke nodded. Sometimes, a patient's emotional state revealed more about her physical well-being than any test or examination was able to reveal. Many doctors failed to realize that. It was a fact that Brooke and Rachel took seriously as an indicator of potential positive or negative outcomes. "Look, Rach. I promise, if anything happens with Daisy I will call you right away." Rachel nodded. "Don't do this to yourself. She's made it this far. Let's hope your gut is wrong. If it is right, I promise you I will do whatever I can to keep that baby right where he or she is for another few weeks."

"I know you will. It's not that. I just can't stand to think what that would do to her. If anything happened now, after so much disappointment…I know she is aware of the risks, but Brooke…"

"Rach, I understand. I like Daisy too. We all do. We all want this to work out. I promise I will review everything again before I leave, okay?"

Rachel nodded again. "Promise me that you will call if you need anything or if anything…"

"I swear."

"It's not just Daisy, Brooke. You have been pulling double duty for a week. God, I have barely passed you in the hallway. You've had back to back patients since Monday and now you are on call."

"I'm fine. If I weren't, I would tell you. Yeah, it's been a hectic week. It happens. Mike was away, you couldn't pick up Regina's load. One day, you'll get stuck covering for me," Brooke said.

Rachel rolled her eyes. "In all these years, you have never once asked me to cover for you." Brooke smiled. "Just call me, if you need me. I know you."

"Then you know that I never break a promise. I said I promise and I do."

"Okay. No offense, I hope I don't hear from you," Rachel admitted.

"None taken. I'll see you Monday," Brooke said.

"Aren't you leaving yet?" Rachel asked.

"After I review this again. Go on. You haven't seen your hubby in days. Go be domestic."

"Are those doctor's orders?" Rachel joked.

"Yep. Need me to write them down?" Brooke asked.

"Jerk," Rachel chuckled. "I'll see you."

Brooke returned her attention to Daisy Menendez's file. She poured through the notes again, committing as much to memory as she could. Rachel was the last person to leave the office. Brooke enjoyed the quiet when everyone had gone home. She reclined in her chair for a moment and closed her eyes. The truth was, she was tired. It was not an unfamiliar feeling, but she was privately hoping for a quiet weekend. She chuckled when she felt the vibration of her pager. *No such luck.*

Tess was enjoying an evening of unusual quiet. Davey was at a friend's birthday sleepover and Dani had fallen asleep earlier than usual. A cold beer and her feet on the couch, listening to a playlist of soft jazz was exactly what she needed. It had seemed to be an exceptionally long week. Davey was just starting baseball. Dani had rehearsals for a dance recital. Her workload had been heavier than normal for the time of year. And, her mother had called insisting that she schedule a vacation and a visit soon. She closed her eyes and let the gentle melodies wash over her. Not so surprisingly, her thoughts traveled to a particular doctor.

She had only crossed paths with Brooke once all week. Brooke had just started to engage her in conversation about the weekend when she was abruptly called away. Brooke had sighed and offered her an apologetic smile. Tess understood. They were both at work and both had a schedule to keep. She wondered if they would ever have an occasion to talk again without being hurried. *Oh, well.* She jumped when her cell phone rang.

"Who could be calling at midnight?" she mused aloud. Tess picked up the unfamiliar number. "Hello? Oh, no. I'm so sorry. Is Davey all right?" Tess felt her heartbeat quicken. "That sick? No, no. I will be right there."

Tess took a deep breath and headed for Dani's room. She shook her daughter softly. "Dani…"

"Mom? What time is it?"

Tess smiled. "It's late. I'm sorry, sweetie. We need to go get your brother at Steven's. He's not feeling well."

"Figures," Dani grumbled.

Tess prodded her daughter a bit. She took a deep breath and grabbed a pair of sweats for Dani. *No rest for the weary.*

"Davey, just try and relax," Tess told her son. Davey was hunched over, holding his stomach tightly.

"I can't. Mom, it hurts," he cried.

"I know, baby. Just try and breathe. We'll be there in a minute."

"I don't want to go to the hospital," he begged.

"I know. We need to figure out what is going on with you. Did you eat something strange? Did you get hit in the stomach or something?" Tess asked as she drove into the emergency room parking lot.

"No. Ugh…Mom. I'm gonna…" Before he could finish his thought, Davey had thrown up all over the backseat.

"Gross," Dani said. Tess shot her daughter a gaze of stern warning. She opened the back door and helped her son out.

Davey's eyes were watering. "Sorry…Mom…I…"

Tess smiled. "It's okay. Come on."

"I don't want to…"

"I know," Tess tried to comfort him. *Oh, God. Please let this be nothing.*

Brooke walked through a set of double doors and into the emergency room waiting area. She heard a slight commotion.

"Mom!" a voice cried out.

"I'm sorry, you can't both go with him," a nurse said.

"I can't leave her out here alone," Tess implored the woman.

Brooke recognized the voice and picked up her pace. She reached Tess just as Davey was being wheeled through another set of doors.

"Mom," he began to cry.

Brooke grabbed hold of Tess's shoulder. When Tess turned, she could see the helpless tears in Tess's eyes. "What's going on?" Brooke asked. Tess shook her head. "Tess?"

"Davey," Tess began. "I don't know what it is…appendicitis. I don't know. He's in so much pain. Throwing up. I have Dani," Tess pointed over to a couch in the waiting area. "They won't let her back there. I can't leave an eight-year-old out here alone," Tess sighed. "What are you doing here?" Tess asked without thinking.

"I work here," Brooke reminded her with a reassuring smile.

"I'm sorry. I just don't know what to do."

Brooke looked over at Dani. "Look, why don't I go see if I can find out where he is right now and what is going on, okay?"

"Brooke, you…"

"Hey, no worries, okay? Let me go see and then we'll figure something out, okay?" Tess nodded. Her tears were surfacing again. "Tess, he'll be fine."

"He's so scared and I am not there."

Brooke understood. "I'll be right back. I promise. Go sit with Dani. She's probably half annoyed and half terrified."

Tess chuckled. "Got her pegged."

"Go on," Brooke instructed her friend. "Be back in a few."

Tess followed Brooke's direction. She felt a small amount of relief knowing that Brooke was checking in on Davey. She still had no idea how she was going to solve her current dilemma. There was no one to call at this hour to watch Dani. She felt like the worst mother on the face of the planet. *What am I supposed to do?*

Brooke strolled through the emergency room purposefully. She stopped and asked the nurse at the desk about

Davey's whereabouts and made her way to the door. She knocked lightly on the door frame. "Knock, knock," she said as she peered in. A young resident turned to face her. Brooke kept her eyes squarely on Davey. The fear in his eyes seemed to lessen slightly when he recognized her face. "Mind if I come in?" she asked. Davey nodded.

Brooke stepped up beside the bed and put her hand on his. "Your mom tells me you're not feeling so hot."

"It hurts," he said.

Brooke nodded and smiled at him. She turned to the resident and extended her hand. "Dr. Bell, I see. We haven't met, I don't believe. I try to stay out of here whenever possible," she confessed with a wink. "Dr. Campbell," Brooke introduced herself.

The young doctor nodded. Almost everyone on staff knew who Brooke Campbell was. It might have sounded ridiculous, and it was a bit uncommon, but the still young OB/GYN was a bit of a legend in this place. Her practice was affiliated with the hospital. When she was on call, she often landed in the emergency department for a consult. Brooke Campbell's ability to deal with difficult patients, get answers, and uncover issues earned her the respect of the staff.

"Dr. Livingston speaks highly of you," he complimented Brooke.

"Does he? I won't tell him you let that slip," she winked. "Would you mind?" she gestured to the boy in the bed.

"Not at all," he said. She looked at Davey's chart and read the initial thoughts of the resident beside her. He had conducted a preliminary exam and had seemingly come to the conclusion that Davey was indeed suffering from appendicitis. Brooke smiled, handed the clipboard back to Dr. Bell and stepped back beside Davey.

"Okay, buddy," she said to him. "I know this super sucks. I'm just gonna poke you a little, okay? You stop me and tell me if it hurts more when I do or when I stop. Okay?" Davey nodded his understanding and Brooke began to gently feel his belly. He winced, but as she would have expected. She smiled at him and continued talking. "What were you doing when you got sick?"

"I was at Steven's."

"Is Steven a friend from school?"

"Yeah," Davey groaned.

"Um. What were you doing at Steven's?"

"Sleepover."

"Um-hum. Jumping around, wrestling, anything like that?" Brooke asked knowingly. Davey shrugged. Brooke tried not to chuckle. "Uh-huh. Anything else?" She noted that Davey turned slightly pale at the question. "Okay, Davey. Listen. You feel awful, right?" He nodded. "I want you to feel better. You want to feel better, don't you?" He nodded again and then grimaced. Brooke folded her arms across her chest. "So, come on. What else did you do? Eat anything that didn't taste right?" she asked him. Davey looked down. "Davey?" she implored him.

Davey sighed. "I don't know what it was."

"You don't know what you ate?" she asked. He shook his head no.

"It was green and gross," he said.

"Like broccoli?" she asked. He shook his head no. "What did it taste like?"

"Green goop."

"What was in the green goop, Davey?"

"I dunno. They dared me to eat it."

Brooke pursed her lips. "Who dared you?"

"The guys. They made it. Truth or dare. It was my dare. I had to eat the whole cup."

Brooke tried to suppress a smile. She leaned into Davey and brushed his sweaty bangs back. "You are going to be fine," she said. "I'm just going to talk to Dr. Bell here in the hallway for a minute, okay? Then I will send your mom back." Davey nodded.

Brooke led the young resident into the hallway. She closed Davey's door and folded her arms again. "What's your diagnosis?" she asked him pointedly.

"Seems clear. Pain on the right side, low-grade fever, nausea, vomiting. Clear cut symptoms of appendicitis."

Brooke pursed her lips again. "Uh-huh. No tenderness or increased pain when I released pressure over the area. Did you ask him about what he had eaten?"

"Yes, of course."

"Um-hum. Did he tell you about his green goop?"

"No…"

"How many times did you ask him?" Brooke pressed.

"I…"

"Dr. Bell, I am going to go out on a limb and make a suggestion to you. Order an X-ray just to be on the safe side, hell, order an ultrasound. Do me a favor? Get a stool sample. Okay? I have a feeling our young friend has food poisoning, not appendicitis."

"Food poisoning? From what?"

"From whatever those boys put in that green goop. I'll see what I can find out about that. I won't share with Dr. Livingston how quickly you were ready to put that boy under a knife."

"Appendicitis can be fatal," he defended himself. "If we don't act and there is a…"

"Surgery can be fatal too," Brooke stopped him. "You don't ever open someone for anything if there is another way, doctor. Rule one. There is no such thing as low-risk surgery," Brooke said.

Dr. Bell swallowed hard. Brooke forced a contrived smile. She was simmering at his arrogance and his ignorance. The only moniker of comfort she gained was in the fact that a staff surgeon would have had to examine Davey before any action was taken.

No matter, his lack of thoroughness angered her. "I'll check in with you in a bit. Who is the doctor on tonight?"

"Dr. Gage," he said with a sigh.

"Good," Brooke said. She nodded to him and headed back toward the waiting area to see Tess. *Of all the stupid, short-sighted, ignorant...* She continued her mental berating of the resident along the way.

Dani was leaning against Tess asleep when Brooke walked into the waiting area. Tess's eyes were closed, but the stress on her features was still evident. Brooke paused for a moment. She couldn't put her finger on what it was about Tess that intrigued her so much. She'd thought about Tess often over the last week. Brooke had been disappointed that she had not gotten to see the courier much during the week. She had hoped that she would be able to casually suggest that they grab a cup of coffee some afternoon. She could use a friend other than Rachel and Tess was easy to talk to. Plus, she was a bit of a puzzle to Brooke. A painter who didn't think she could paint, a single mom who once thought she would be a doctor, a fairly young single mom who was a lesbian, Brooke was curious about all of it. And, there was the fact that she found Tess attractive. Brooke had no intention of acting on any attraction she might feel toward her new friend. That had only one place to lead—disaster. She would prefer a long-term friendship over a short-term romance, and Brooke could not envision herself in anything long-term in the romance department.

Her breath caught slightly as she approached the pair on the long couch in the waiting room. She had only seen Tess out of uniform once. Everything had happened so quickly that night and there had been so much excitement with the kids, that Brooke did not pay that much attention. She seemed to recall that Tess had been wearing jeans and a blouse. Now, Tess was stretched out in a pair of faded jeans, a plain blue T-shirt, and a well-worn, bright purple, pair of Nike sneakers. Her hair was down, not pulled up or back as it usually was. Brooke noticed for the first time the chestnut color and the soft wave to Tess's hair.

Tess felt someone's gaze upon her. She opened her eyes nervously and was met with a comforting smile from Brooke. "Hey, there," Brooke said softly.

"Hey. Is he.."

Brooke smiled a bit broader. "He's okay. I'm not a hundred percent sure, but I would bet when the tests come back we are going to see that he has food poisoning."

"What?" Tess asked in surprise. "He was at a pizza party," she said in disbelief. "See? I told you that slimy meat is not a good idea."

Brooke couldn't help but chuckle. "I don't think it was the pizza. Probably not cake or ice cream or any of the snacks at the party either."

"But, I sent him to school with lunch. Oh, no…Do you think that…"

"Relax," Brooke said. "Unless you sent him with some concoction he calls green goop, I think you can rest easy that your lunch was not the culprit."

"Green goop? Why do I suddenly think I do not want to know?" Tess asked cautiously.

Brooke shrugged. "Truth or dare. He took the dare."

"I'll kill him," Tess said with a roll of her eyes.

Brooke laughed. "I think he's learned his lesson. It would help if we had some idea what his friends gave him, though. Just to be on the safe side. I have some suspicions, but just to be sure."

"I'll call Steven's mom," Tess said. "What were they thinking?"

"They weren't. They're eight," Brooke said.

Tess sighed. "I am so sorry you got dragged into this. This is not exactly your problem or your…"

"That's what friends are for," Brooke said as a matter of fact. Tess smiled. "Look, why don't you call his friend's mom. Then go back and see Davey for a bit. He's on an IV for fluids. He'll need that for a bit to get him hydrated."

"Dani…I can't leave…"

"Well, I have a patient I want to check on. I'll do that while you call. When I get back, I can take Dani down to the cafeteria with me. They don't have much this time of night, but I could use a coffee and she could probably use a change of scenery."

"Brooke, I…"

"Make your call," Brooke said. "I'll be back in about fifteen minutes."

Tess nodded. She watched Brooke head back through the emergency room double doors and pulled her phone from her pocket. *Thank God she was here. What the hell did you get into, Davey?*

"How are you doing?" Brooke asked Daisy Menendez. Rachel's gut had turned out to be right on the money and Daisy had begun to go into premature labor. Brooke had managed to stop it in its tracks for the time being.

"Terrified," Daisy admitted.

Brooke nodded her understanding. "I know you are. You need to try and relax, Daisy. Try and relax, okay? Believe it or not that is the best thing you can do for both you and this baby. You are 35 weeks in. I'd like to get you to hang in there at least one more—at least. You need to try and stay calm. Everything with the baby looks good. Okay? There is a great team here, and I don't just mean Dr. Cantrell and our group. Terrific pediatricians and specialists that are prepared if this little one is determined to get here early."

"Dr. Campbell, I…If this is because of something…"

"You have done everything right. People's bodies are different, that's all. Trust me. Try and get some sleep. Right now, everything looks good," Brooke said.

"How long am I going to be here?" Daisy asked.

Brooke took a deep breath. Ultimately, Rachel would make that call. Brooke suspected that Rachel would agree with her assessment. She did not want to cause Daisy any stress at the moment. "Let's get through the weekend. I'll talk to Dr. Cantrell. We'll see how things look Monday and go from there. Okay?" Daisy nodded. "Get some rest," Brooke said softly before making her way out of the room to go check on a much younger patient.

She heard Davey crying from the hallway and stepped into the room to find the same resident standing at his bedside. "What's going on?" she demanded a bit more harshly than was her usual nature.

"I want Mom," Davey said.

Brooke stepped up to the bed and accepted him into a hug. Eight was a unique age. Davey was caught between wanting to seem grown up and wanting his mommy. He was sick. He was in a strange place and he was scared. "Mom will be back here in a few minutes," Brooke promised. "I just had to do a couple of things first."

"Brooke?"

"Yeah, buddy?"

"Am I gonna die?"

Brooke looked at the resident with daggers. *What the hell did you say to this kid?* "Davey, I told you, you are going to be fine."

"Then why do I have to stay here? I want to go home."

"I know. I know you do. Let me talk to Dr. Bell, okay? Do you still feel sick?"

Davey shook his head no. "Just my stomach aches now."

"I gave him something for nausea," Dr. Bell said.

Brooke gave him a disgusted smile. *Oh, well, let's get you a medal for that.* "Try and close your eyes for a bit, okay?" she said to Davey.

"It itches."

"What itches?" Brooke asked him.

"My arm," Davey said.

Brooke looked at the small catheter in Davey's arm. The site was a bit redder than usual. She shook her head. "That's just for fluids. When you throw up so much, you get dehydrated."

"What's that?" he asked.

Brooke was simmering again. He was eight, not stupid. "It means you lose water in your body. You need that water. That's all. Okay? I'm going to step out. In a few minutes, your mom will be here, all right?"

Davey nodded. "Brooke?"

"Yeah?"

"I'm still scared."

Brooke ruffled Davey's hair slightly. "Nothing to be scared of."

"Some guy was screaming," he said.

Brooke struggled not to sigh and then scream. This is why children's hospitals were best for children. The emergency department on a Friday night could get crazy, loud, and frightening for an adult. "It's okay. I promise you are safe. I promise," she assured him. He nodded with still wide eyes.

Brooke hated leaving, but she knew she had to get Tess to Davey, and soon. She led the resident into the hall. "So, what's the verdict?"

"You were right. I just saw his mother. We'll admit him for the night."

"Is that really necessary?" Brooke asked.

"I think so," he said indignantly.

You would, you little asswipe. "I see. Well, I have a make and then I will send his mom back here. I assume you are getting him a room?"

"Well, we will try. You know how it is…"

Brooke leaned into the young resident's face and held his gaze. "You admit that little boy, you had damn well better find him a room." She stepped back and headed down the hallway deliberately. She stopped just shy of the double doors and stepped into an empty examination room. "Fuck," she grumbled in frustration as she grabbed her cell phone.

"Brooke?" Rachel answered sleepily. "Oh, God…Daisy…Did she…"

"Daisy is okay, Rach. I've got her on Betamethasone."

"You think she's going to deliver," Rachel said.

"Not immediately, no. I think she might in the next week if we can't keep her relaxed. And, I'd like to do everything we can to have that baby's lungs in the best shape we can if she does. Right now? Right now, she is hanging in there. I don't expect any issues as long as she is here and being quiet and monitored."

"Good. What is it then? I can hear it in your voice. Something is wrong."

Brooke sighed heavily. "Rach, I hate to ask this. I really do…"

"What is it?"

"I need you to cover me this weekend, well at least until tomorrow afternoon."

"Are you okay?" Rachel sat straight up in bed. Brooke never asked for help, never.

"I'm okay. It's Tess, actually."

"Tess?"

"Well, actually it's Davey, Tess's son," Brooke explained. explained.

Rachel was confused. The concern in Brooke's voice was genuine. It was also palpable. Brooke was upset. "Whatever you need, Brooke. You know that. Is her son..."

"She brought him in earlier. Jesus, sometimes I hate this place," Brooke admitted in frustration.

Rachel sucked in a ragged breath. There were only two times she could recall hearing the tone she heard in Brooke's voice now. Once, when a nurse had given the wrong meds to one of her patients and nearly killed her. The other when Brooke's father had his heart attack two years ago. "Brooke?"

"He's all right. No thanks to the idiot resident treating him. Food poisoning. Poor kid is terrified in here. Tess is stuck in the waiting room because she has Dani."

Rachel groaned audibly. How strict rules were adhered to depended on the time of day. Late on a Friday night was one of those times when rules were seldom bent. "Shit," she said.

"Yeah. Tell me. Anyway, this asshole kid wants to admit him."

"Does he need that?" Rachel asked.

"No, but I am betting Gage will back him unless someone is there to watch Davey. And, honestly? I don't think Tess should drive anyway. She's a wreck and exhausted. Plus, apparently Davey puked in the backseat. That will not be good if I can get him out of here," Brooke explained.

Rachel's lips turned up into a smile. Brooke liked Tess. As compassionate as Brooke was, this went far beyond empathy. "I'll call the service. Do you need me there now?" Rachel asked.

“No, I checked on Daisy just now. Mrs. Brennan delivered at eight. No other calls—yet.”

“Okay, Just go take care of Tess and Davey,” Rachel said intentionally. She was curious to see how Brooke would react.

“Thanks, Rach. You should have seen his face. No for a kid if he doesn’t have to be here. Tess is…You know, she feels guilty because she has Dani, but…Anyway, I just want to get them out of here.”

Rachel nodded on the other end of the phone. “You’re going to stay with them?”

“Tess has a couch, so yeah, if that’s what it takes.”

“Let me know how it works out,” Rachel said.

“I will. Tell Mike I am sorry for screwing up your weekend.”

“He’ll understand.”

“I’d better go. I don’t want Davey alone in there too long.”

“You go. I’ll talk to you,” Rachel said as she hung up the call. “I’ll be damned,” she said in awe.

“What happened?” Mike asked.

“Brooke needs me to cover this weekend.”

“Is she okay?” Mike sat up beside his wife.

“Yeah. Unless, falling for someone is a bad thing,” Rachel laughed.

“Huh? Brooke’s in love?’

“No. Not love. Definitely like. She is definitely in like and for Brooke? Well…”

“I don’t get it, but…”

“I’ll explain tomorrow. Unless, of course, I am delivering a baby,” Rachel said as she laid back down.

“Umm,” Mike yawned. “Does that mean I don’t have to mow the lawn now that I have Eli by myself?”

“Guess again, Mr. I Needed a Ride-On Mower.”

“Great.”

Chapter Four

Brooke managed to catch Dr. Paul Gage before heading to get Tess. She had not intended to send the young resident, Dr. Bell up the river, but once their conversation began, she felt she had no choice. It was one thing to be inexperienced or even a bit arrogant. It was completely unacceptable to put your arrogance and pride over a patient's welfare. Brooke had reached her limit. She preferred to be approachable and mild-mannered in her interactions. When necessary, she could be assertive, even aggressive. She reserved that part of her personality for occasions that warranted it. That had served her well. When she did speak with stoic authority, people took notice.

Tess stood the moment she saw Brooke approaching. Dani was sound asleep on the couch. "They want to admit him," Tess said helplessly. Brooke smiled. "What am I going to do?"

Brooke gestured for Tess to sit back down and promptly took a seat beside her. "That depends."

"On what? Brooke, I can't have Dani…"

"Tess! Calm down, okay?"

"I'm sorry."

Brooke smiled. "You have nothing to be sorry for. Look, they are afraid to let him go because of dehydration. He's not feeling as sick because of the meds. That doesn't mean his stomach can tolerate anything yet. That's why he has the IV." Tess nodded sadly. "I spoke to the supervising doctor. He assured me that if we can get Davey to sip some water and hold it down, they will release him." Tess began to smile. "If…If someone is there to watch him that knows what to look for."

"I…."

"Tess," Brooke hesitated. For some reason, she was afraid to continue.

"Brooke? What?"

"Look, I can take you guys home. If he can keep a bit down, then I can watch him. They'll release him if..."

"I can't ask you to do that," Tess said.

"You didn't. I offered."

"Aren't you working? What if you need to..."

"Rachel's got that covered." Tess stared dumbfounded at Brooke. "I'm not trying to put you on the spot. I just know he's scared. You're exhausted. You need sleep, all of you. You can do that at home."

"So do you," Tess observed. She looked in Brooke's eyes and struggled to breathe.

Brooke chuckled. "I was on call anyway. I'm used to it."

"Brooke...You hardly know us. I can't ask you..."

"Again, you didn't. Let me help. I can. I want to," Brooke said honestly. Tess felt a tear fall across her cheek. "Hey, no crying," Brooke said. "Come on, you go on in and see Davey. I will stay with Dani until they give the okay. All right?"

"Who are you?" Tess asked.

"I hope your friend," Brooke answered.

"Me too," Tess said.

"Go," Brooke said. "Have Dr. Bell page me when Davey is ready to go."

Tess walked away and through the double doors in a daze. Everything in Brooke's demeanor was sincere. Tess couldn't fathom why the doctor would go out of her way for Tess's family. She had to accept. She needed to accept. More than that, she wanted to accept Brooke's help. It felt good to have a friend. Brooke cared what happened. That was evident. Tess sighed. *Probably the doctor in her.* She thought back to what Janine had told her about Dr. Brooke Campbell. *She's a rare breed.* "That, she most definitely is," Tess mused as she walked into Davey's room.

"Mom!"

"Hey, sweetie," Tess made her way to her son. He promptly grabbed hold of her.

"I don't want to stay here," he cried.

"I know you don't, baby," Tess said. Her heart ached. She could feel Davey's fear. "Brooke is working on that."

"She is?"

"Yeah. She is," Tess said. Davey snuggled against her. She felt his tears through her T-shirt. "It's okay now," she assured him. "I'm not leaving you again."

"Where's Dani?" he asked through a sob.

Tess closed her eyes. "She's with Brooke."

"Can we go home now?" he asked.

"In a while, baby. First, you need to drink something. Okay?"

He nodded against Tess and held onto her. "I hate it here."

"I know. I hate you being here." Tess sat on the bed and held Davey close. She rocked him gently as she did when he was an infant, hoping he would rest until the doctor came in to see if he could drink some water. "Rest, sweetheart. I'm right here. We'll go home soon." Tess closed her eyes. She had heard what Brooke said. Somehow, she was certain that Davey would be going home shortly. There was a hint of something other than compassion in Brooke's eyes. Fire, that was what Tess saw. It was faint, a slight glow that flickered behind Brooke's gentleness. Tess made a note to delve into that at some point. *A friend. I hope so, Brooke. I hope so.*

Brooke lifted Davey from the backseat of her SUV and followed Tess into the house. Tess directed her to Davey's bedroom while she helped prod a sleepy Dani into her room. "I'll be right there," Tess told Brooke.

Brooke nodded and continued into Davey's room. She set him down on the bed and he rubbed his eyes. "Mom?"

"Sorry, buddy, no. She'll be right here," Brooke said.

"Brooke?" he asked in sleepy confusion.

"Yep. Fraid so, buddy," she said as she took a seat on the edge of his bed. "How do you feel?"

"Tired," he moaned.

Brooke smiled. "I'll bet. You had an eventful night."

"Mom told the doctor what they put in that stuff," Davey said.

"Yeah, I know."

"The guys are gonna hate me. You're not supposed to squeal."

Tess was making her way into the room and stopped outside Davey's door when she heard him speaking to Brooke.

Brooke took a deep breath. "Nah, they won't hate you."

"Will too," he said sadly.

"No, buddy. They won't. I promise. You were really sick, D." Davey smiled at the tall doctor. "What?" Brooke asked.

"You called me D. That's what the guys call me."

Brooke smiled. "Well, you seem a little big to be Davey all the time." Davey smiled and yawned. "You need to get some rest," Brooke said. "In a little while, I will wake you up to drink something."

Davey nodded and closed his eyes. Brooke thought he was asleep and started to leave. Davey grabbed her hand and stopped her. "I'm glad you are Mom's friend," he said. Brooke looked at him curiously. "She needs a friend," he said sleepily.

Brooke nodded as he drifted off to sleep. *So do I, D. So do I.*

Tess came down the stairs and found Brooke in the kitchen filling the tea kettle. "I hope you don't mind," Brooke said.

"Not at all."

"I picked some tea up when we stopped at the pharmacy," Brooke said. "Sometimes, it relaxes me." Tess nodded and collapsed into a kitchen chair. She put her face in her hands and sighed. "You okay?" Brooke asked.

"Yeah."

"You mind if I tell you that I think you are full of shit?" Brooke asked lightly.

Tess looked up in surprise. When she saw Brooke with her arms folded across her chest, she chuckled. "You adding counselor to the list of roles you played tonight?" Tess joked.

"I have no idea what you are talking about," Brooke said.

"Let's see…Doctor, babysitter, personal shopper, chauffer, what else…"

"How about just a friend?" Brooke said.

Tess smiled and sighed. "I don't have many of those these days."

"Neither do I," Brooke confessed. "Well, there is Rach. She is a royal pain in my ass half the time, but she is my best friend."

"Yeah. You're lucky. Most of mine vanished when I had Dani and Davey. You find out who your real friends are in times like that." The kettle started to whistle and Brooke grabbed hold of it. "In the right-hand cupboard," Tess pointed.

"Care to join me?" Brooke asked. Tess nodded. "Well, good. I was going to ask you to have coffee this week. It just got crazy. I can't say this is what I had envisioned," Brooke said as she made them each a cup of tea.

"That seems to happen a lot to us," Tess said.

"Maybe it's fate," Brooke said, placing a steaming mug in front of Tess.

"Maybe," Tess replied. "Thanks," she said softly.

Brooke saw the tears begin to roll down Tess's cheeks. "It's just tea," she said lightly.

Tess looked up. "No. It really isn't."

Brooke took a deep breath. She meant what she had said about being Tess's friend. There was something about Tess that pulled her toward the woman. It was strange to Brooke. As much as she found Tess attractive, the connection she felt was somehow deeper. She wasn't interested in trying to get Tess into bed. At least, that wasn't all she was interested in. She wanted to get to know Tess. She wanted to spend time with her. *Oh shit. Am I actually thinking about pursuing a relationship? No. Bad idea, Campbell. Bad idea.*

"Tess," Brooke called softly. Tess shook her head. "Talk to me. That's what friends do, right?" *Jesus, did that just come out of my mouth?*

Tess looked up again. "Davey and Dani were a surprise."

"I sort of gathered that," Brooke admitted.

Tess grinned uncomfortably. "I had been with Daniel since the seventh grade. I never dreamed he would bag on us." Brooke listened silently. "He did. Asshole." Brooke chuckled slightly at the word as it rolled off Tess's tongue. Tess smiled and shrugged. "Well, he is! I would say that my life would have been simpler if I had realized I was a lesbian sooner. Maybe it would have been. Who knows? I wouldn't have Dani and Davey, and I would never change that. Not for anything."

Brooke smiled. She had no doubt of the sincerity of Tess's declaration. She'd seen it as clear as day all evening long. Dani and Davey were the center of Tess's life. That was obvious. "So, you were in college then?"

"Yeah. My junior year. It sucked. Everyone was against me going through with it. Daniel, my parents…"

"You mean your pregnancy?"

"Yeah," Tess said in disgust. It still left a bitter taste in her mouth. "The thing is, from the moment I found out I was pregnant, that was my baby. My baby. Not a fetus. Not an inconvenience. Turned out to be a little more than I bargained for," Tess chuckled.

"Twins, you mean?" Brooke guessed.

"Uh-huh. How that happened…"

"Well, they are fraternal so…" Tess laughed at Brooke's inclination to explain in doctor mode. "Sorry," Brooke said. "Force of habit."

"No, it's cute," Tess said without thinking. *Oh my God! Did I just say that out loud? To Brooke? Oh my God. Shoot me. Please? Now.*

Brooke blushed. "Continue with your story," she said quietly as she sipped her tea.

"Well, long story short, I wanted them. I really did. It was really hard for a long time. My parents were not happy. Daniel skipped out. I mean, he literally skipped out. I don't even know where he is. That's how far he ran."

Brooke shook her head. She had seen that more than once and it utterly confounded her. How any parent could not want to be a part of a child's life was beyond her comprehension. Even after her parents had split and moved to separate coasts, Brooke's father always stayed in contact. He always made sure he spent time with Brooke, even if it was never as much or the way she would have liked. "I'm sorry," Brooke said.

"Don't be. The hardest part was leaving school."

"Do you ever think about going back?" Brooke wondered.

"I do. Someday I will," Tess said. "I think so. Not now. They need me. I took a full-time job and lived with my grandmother for three years until I saved enough money to buy this house. Then, I met Jackie. She was home when I was working. It worked until it didn't work anymore for her," Tess said.

Brooke wanted Tess to continue, but she didn't want to press. "You don't have to talk about this. Not now, anyway."

"It's okay. It's the past. Jackie was Jackie. She was my first, you know?" Tess confessed. Brooke smiled. "It was just too much for her, I think. We were young. She was a year younger than me, only twenty-four with two kids. She just wasn't ready. I get it. The kids didn't."

"She doesn't see them?"

"No. After two years, she left. Not sure what ended up happening. She was with someone for a while. I never tried to stay in touch. If you have to force it...Well, you shouldn't have to force it." Brooke agreed. "By the time she left, the kids were going into first grade. I had worked my way up. They go to a before school program and an after school program. I am able to pick them up by four-thirty and have dinner with them. I don't work weekends. It works for all of us. So, that's my not so sad story," Tess laughed. "I don't regret it. Not any of it. I just wish I could give them more. Like tonight. God, poor Davey. It's so hard. My parents are in Florida. My gram in gone. Just...sometimes it's overwhelming. I wonder if I am failing them."

Brooke shook her head. She was constantly surrounded by parents and families. Some were expecting for the first time. Some were couples. Some were alone. Some had large families already. She had a good sense of who and how parents were. Tess was an exceptional mother. Her kids came first. She loved them unconditionally. She provided structure and love. Brooke didn't need one more second in Tess's company to know that. "I'd say they are lucky to have you," Brooke told her friend.

"They deserve more than I can give them sometimes," Tess said.

"I doubt they see it that way," Brooke said. "I see lots of kids and parents, Tess. Trust me on this one. You remind me of my mom," Brooke said.

"Oh, no. That doesn't sound like a good thing."

Brooke laughed. "No, it is. My mom is the best person I know."

"So, you are close?"

"Yeah. Wish we saw each other more," Brooke confessed.

"Is she far away?"

"No, not really. She teaches at The University of Connecticut."

"Wow. What does she teach?"

Brooke scrunched her face uncomfortably. "Orthopedic surgery techniques."

"Your mom is a surgeon?"

"Both my parents are. Technically, my mom is a professor now. She stopped practicing when she left my dad. I was twelve."

Tess detected a note of sadness in Brooke's voice. "Is that what made you want to be a doctor? Your parents?"

Brooke sighed. "Partly. My dad just retired last year after he had a heart attack. He lives in California. My mom, she was a gifted surgeon. People still seek her out for advice. She's sort of a champion of women in medicine. She was a woman in a field where there weren't many women at the time. There still aren't. She's a talented doctor and teacher by all accounts," Brooke said proudly. "But, she was an even better mom."

"She sounds amazing."

"She is. She gave up surgery when we moved to this coast. She was a single mom. The hours were too much. You know?" Brooke said.

Tess watched Brooke carefully. She sensed that Brooke felt a sense of guilt in her mother's transition. "Hum. I do know.

I never really thought of leaving school as giving anything up. I mean, I just made a change."

"Because you had to," Brooke pointed out.

Tess shook her head. "No, I wanted to. I could've gone back to school. I could now."

"You don't want to?"

"I do, but I want to spend time with my kids more. School will be there in five, ten or fifteen years. Davey and Dani will only be kids for a while. I don't know. Sometimes I wonder what it would have been like if I had just stayed that original course, but then I look at them and that doesn't seem to matter. I didn't plan on being a mom on my twenty-first birthday," Tess laughed. "But, sometimes the best things happen when you don't plan them." Tess yawned.

Brooke smiled at her friend. Tess was exhausted. "You need some sleep," Brooke observed.

"Is that your professional opinion, Dr. Campbell?" Tess asked a bit flirtatiously.

"It is a personal diagnosis, Ms. Sinclair," Brooke replied.

Tess nodded. "You can have the bed. The couch pulls out. I'll just get a sheet..."

Brooke grabbed Tess's hand. "No. I need to go wake Davey and get him to drink something first. You go to bed," Brooke said.

"My bedroom is next to Davey's. You'll be closer there," Tess argued.

"Somehow, I think you would feel better if you were next door to him. And, I am not putting you on the couch, Tess. Besides, I sleep on couches all the time."

"Not in this house, Dr. Campbell," Tess said. Brooke pursed her lips in amusement. "You can either take the whole bed or you can take the right side. You choose. You're not sleeping on a couch after the night we have all had," Tess said definitively. Brooke smirked. "Well? Get his drink and let's go," Tess ordered.

"I thought the doctor was supposed to give the orders?" Brooke poked.

"Am I your patient?" Tess asked.

"No."

"Then, my house—my orders. You go wake up Davey and I will get you something to sleep in. Although, my sweats might be shorts on you," Tess laughed.

"Tess, you don't have to..."

"God, you really are determined, aren't you?" Tess said. "You are not going to win this one, doc," Tess said as she headed for the stairs. "Can't say as I have had a sleepover recently, but what the hell!"

Brooke snickered and went to get Davey some Pedialyte. *You might be in trouble here, Campbell. Triple trouble.*

Tess popped her head into Davey's room. He was groggy and she heard Brooke snicker at his sleepy talk.

"Bluck," he complained.

"It's strawberry," Brooke laughed.

"Eww..."

"This from the boy who eats green goop?" Brooke teased Davey.

Davey groaned again. "I'm tired."

"I know, Buddy. Want me to tell you a secret?" Brooke whispered. Davey nodded. "I'm kind of tired too," she pulled the cup away and smiled at him. "That's enough, I think. Do you need to go to the bathroom?" Davey shook his head. "Okay. Go to sleep," Brooke said. Davey was asleep as soon as his head hit the pillow again. Brooke smiled down at him. *I wish I could do that.*

Tess leaned on the doorframe. "Okay, sleepyhead, your turn to hit the pillow," Tess said. Brooke turned. Tess chuckled at the alarmed expression on the doctor's face. "Well? Come on. I think I might have found something to fit you."

Brooke dutifully followed Tess into Tess's bedroom. She watched as Tess reached over onto the bed and retrieved a large pair of sweat pants and an oversized T-shirt. Tess handed the items to Brooke and Brooke laughed. "Did you date the Jolly Green Giant or something?" Brooke asked playfully.

"Ha-ha. Believe it or not those are my brother's. He left them here when he visited last summer." Tess looked Brooke up and down. "I'd say you two are about the same," she paused for effect. "Height."

"Nice save, Sinclair." Brooke responded.

"Bathroom is right there. I left a toothbrush out for you," Tess said with a sly grin.

"Thanks," Brooke said suspiciously as she headed for the bathroom.

Brooke had to admit that she was relieved to be stepping into a soft pair of sweats. She was no stranger to sleeping in her clothes, but she always slept better when she was able to relax. Wearing the clothes she worked in never helped in that endeavor. And, relaxing was always a challenge for Brooke in the best of circumstances. She stretched her back until it popped gently and made her way to the sink. "The Hulk?" Brooke chuckled at the green toothbrush with a Hulk handle that Tess had left out for her. "I swear if this toothpaste is bubble gum flavor," she shook her head.

Tess took the opportunity that Brooke's absence afforded her and slipped into her pajamas. *Well, you won't have to worry about attracting her once she sees your night attire.* Tess heard the door to the bathroom open and turned to find a refreshed Brooke holding up her special toothbrush. Brooke's plan to tease Tess over the toothbrush flew out the window when she saw Tess in her pajamas. Brooke's eyes roamed over Tess and her eyebrows rose almost into her hairline.

"What?" Tess asked defensively. Brooke pursed her lips and shook her head. "Do you have something against Wonder Woman?" Tess blinked her eyelashes.

Brooke cleared her throat and held up her small toothbrush. "Umm…Tess, is there something you would like to tell me?"

"What do you mean?"

"Well, you just had me swap spit with The Hulk and you apparently want me to share a bed with Wonder Woman..." Before Brooke could finish her statement, she was hit in the chest with a flying pillow. "Violence is not the answer, Ms. Sinclair. Don't make me angry, you wouldn't like me when I'm angry," Brooke warned sternly, toothbrush in hand.

"Ooohh…Am I supposed to be scared?" Tess asked.

"You forget, Ms. Sinclair, David Banner was a doctor too. Until, that is, his experiments went wildly wrong."

"He was a scientist," Tess rolled her eyes.

"Same difference," Brooke replied with a sneer.

Tess leveled a defiant gaze at her friend. "Well, Dr. Banner, the right side is yours," Tess grinned. She climbed into the bed and arched her brow at Brooke to follow. Brooke grabbed the pillow at her feet and climbed onto the bed. "I knew I bought a king size bed for a reason," Tess mumbled as she shut out the light.

"What?" Brooke asked.

"Well, should you morph into some large, green creature in the middle of the night, at least I will still have leg room," Tess said with a yawn.

Brooke chuckled. "You're a bit touched, aren't you?" she asked affectionately.

"Not lately," Tess replied. Brooke swallowed hard. "Goodnight, Brooke. I mean, Dr. Banner."

"Goodnight, Tess. I mean, Diana," Brooke yawned.

"Thanks," Tess whispered.

"Don't thank me yet. I hog the covers," Brooke answered. Tess smiled and let herself begin to drift off to sleep. Brooke looked over at her new friend in the faint light. *Why do I have a feeling that lasso of truth is going to get me in trouble? Triple trouble.* Brooke took a deep breath and closed her eyes. For the first time in months, she felt herself slip into a calm and restful sleep.

Chapter Five

Brooke woke up with a sliver of sunlight warming her face. It took her a moment to remember where she was. She rolled to her side and came face to face with a sleeping Tess. Brooke smiled at the contentment on the younger woman's features. It had been many years since she had shared a bed with another woman solely out of friendship and without expectation. In fact, Brooke realized as she watched Tess sleeping, that the last woman she slept beside without engaging in any physical exploration had been Rachel. That had been over seven years ago. Back then, it was a frequent occurrence more out of necessity and exhaustion than anything else.

Tess looked peaceful and relaxed. The expression on her face stood in stark contrast to the worry and guilt that had painted circles under Tess's eyes the night before. Brooke shifted carefully, not wanting to disturb her friend. She glanced to her right and noted the time. *Holy crap! It's after nine.* Brooke never slept past six in the morning. Even when she was sick or had been up for hours, Brooke's inner clock always jarred her from sleep early. She attributed that to two things. The first was her many years of rising before the sun to get in a workout before school or rounds. The second was the numerous cat naps she sometimes took when she was on call. Five hours of solid sleep was a monumental achievement for Brooke. The sun had almost been ready to rise when she and Tess had climbed under the covers. Brooke laughed softly. *Wonder Woman needs some more nap time.*

It didn't surprise Brooke that the rest of the Sinclair clan was also still in dreamland. She poked her head into Dani's room and laughed softly at the girl who had kicked the covers completely off her bed. Dani was clinging to a pillow wrapped in a Wonder Woman pillow case that nearly matched her mother's pajamas. Brooke left the room chuckling and made her way to Davey's door. She gently felt his head and was pleased to see that he had remained cool. There was also markedly more color in his cheeks than there had been a few hours earlier. Just as she was about to leave the room, he stirred.

"Mom?" he called hoarsely.

"No. Sorry, D."

Davey sat up and rubbed his eyes. "I'm thirsty."

"I'll bet," Brooke replied. "Do you want me to get you something or do you want to come downstairs with me?"

"You slept over?" he asked.

Brooked nodded. She wasn't certain how the young boy might perceive that fact. "I wanted to make sure you were okay," she explained.

Davey rubbed his eyes again and nodded. "My stomach feels funny."

"It probably will for a while," Brooke admitted. "Do you think that maybe you could try some toast or something plain?" she asked him. He wrinkled his nose but nodded. "Okay. Maybe you can help me find things," Brooke suggested.

Davey stretched and moved slowly from the bed. He looked at Brooke curiously. "Where's Mom?"

"Still sleeping. What do you say we let her do that for a while longer?"

"Yeah. She never sleeps," he commented innocently.

Another thing we apparently have in common.

Tess awoke to the distant smell of coffee and the faint sound of soft laughter. She stretched in her bed and yawned before rolling to her side to check the time. An unfamiliar scent wafted from the pillow beside her and Tess closed her eyes. *Brooke.* Tess pulled the pillow to her and inhaled deeply. She had not shared her bed with anyone since Jackie, except occasionally when one of her children crawled in beside her after a nightmare or being sick. What surprised her the most was the level of comfort she felt with Brooke beside her. It never occurred to her that Brooke would attempt to take advantage of the situation. In fact, she was positive that even if she had wanted Brooke to do just that, Brooke would have declined. *This is not good.* Tess breathed in deeply again. *Just friends, Tess. That's what you need, a friend. Not a friend with benefits, a friend.* A burst of laughter from below jarred Tess from her musings. *What are those two up to?* She climbed from the bed reluctantly and looked at the time on the clock. *Ten-thirty? It can't be. How did I sleep so late?* Slowly, Tess made her way down the stairs. She was straining to hear the conversation that was taking place a few rooms away.

"How come they look like that?" Dani asked.

"I don't know. I read the instructions," Brooke answered smartly.

"Mom never reads the instructions," Davey said taking a small bite from his piece of toast.

"No? How does she make them?" Brooke asked. Dani looked at the uneven plop that Brooke had in the pan and wrinkled her nose.

Davey shrugged. "She just knows stuff, I guess."

"I'll bet she can't deliver a baby," Brooke muttered.

"Well, that depends on what you mean. I did manage these two," Tess said from behind Brooke. Brooke spun on her heels. The look on the doctor's face was priceless. Tess closed the distance between them and looked over Brooke's shoulder at the contents of the pan on the stove. "Interesting," she commented playfully.

"I read the directions," Brooke said softly.

Tess detected the embarrassment and a touch of disappointment in Brooke's voice and decided that teasing her would have to wait for another time. She was touched by the attempt Brooke had made. Tess didn't need to spend another moment with Brooke to understand that domesticity was not the doctor's forte. She squeezed Brooke's shoulder gently. "Pancakes are trickier than they look," she said sweetly.

Brooke sighed. She was not used to failure. This felt like an epic failure to her. *Jesus, Campbell, you can't even make pancakes! You operate on people for God's sake! How hard can it be?*

"Brooke," Tess said softly.

Brooke shook her head in frustration. "I'm sorry," Brooke said dejectedly.

Tess pulled the doctor to face her and smiled. "For making coffee? Feeding my kids? Letting me sleep? Which thing are you apologizing for?" she asked.

"I wanted to do something nice for you," Brooke said. Her voice was so soft that it left Tess wondering if Brooke had meant to speak the words out loud at all. "The coffee is edible. I swear," Brooke added.

Tess giggled. "Go sit down. Let me do this. You've done too much already," she said.

"I…"

"Go. My house, my orders. Remember?" Tess teased.

Brooke managed a small smile. She made her way to the coffee maker and poured Tess a cup of coffee. "I don't know how you take it," she said. *This is bizarre. I feel like we've known each other so much longer. I don't even know how you take your coffee.*

"Just milk," Tess told her. Brooke added some milk to the cup and handed it to Tess. "Thanks," Tess said. "Go and relax. How long have you been up?"

"A little over an hour," Brooke said.

"Why didn't you wake me up?"

"Brooke said we should let you sleep," Davey explained.

Tess looked at Brooke gratefully. She was about to say thank you when Brooke's phone began ringing. "Sorry," Brooke said as she lifted it.

"Brooke?" Rachel's voice came over the line.

"Yeah."

"You okay?" Rachel asked.

"Yeah, fine. Why?" Brooke wondered. "Is everything all right? Do you need me?"

Rachel chuckled. "No, Dr. Wonderful. Believe it or not, I remember how to deliver babies all by myself," Rachel replied.

"How's Daisy doing?"

"The same," Rachel said. "Are you home?"

"No," Brooke said as she watched Davey toss a piece of toast at his sister. *Oh boy, he is starting to feel better.* "We were just having breakfast."

Rachel held her cell phone away from her and looked at it as if it had grown a head. She mentally shook herself before replacing it to her ear. "How is Tess's son?"

"Better," Brooke said with a slight chuckle. She could feel Davey and Dani leg wrestling under the table. *Definitely better.* "Listen, I can take over now. You don't have to work the whole weekend."

"No. You must be tired. It was late when you called last night," Rachel said. "It's fine."

"Actually, I slept really well," Brooke said without thinking. For the second time in a few minutes, Rachel looked at her phone in disbelief. "I do have to get Tess to her car at some point."

"Just do what you need to do," Rachel said. "I was just checking in."

"Call me if you need me," Brooke said as a smiling Tess placed a plate of pancakes in front of her.

"Yeah. Okay. I'll see you Monday then," Rachel said.

"Sounds good," Brooke replied. "Thanks, Rach."

"Anytime," Rachel said as she hung up the phone. *What is going on with you, Brooke?*

"Everything okay?" Tess asked.

"Yep," Brooke answered.

"Listen, you don't need to get me to the car. I can call…"

The truth was that Brooke did not want her time with Tess to end. It seemed crazy to think that she was having fun. *Only you would find puking children, strange houses, chaste sleepovers, and embarrassing breakfast a source of fun, Campbell. Only you.* "If you would rather call someone else…"

"No," Tess responded more quickly that she would have liked and blushed. "It's not that," she said. "You just have gone out of your way already. I'm sure you have things you would rather be doing."

Not really, no. "I could be roaming the hospital hallways," Brooke said. "Jay is looking in on Murphy. So, no big deal," she downplayed the situation as much as she could.

"Who is Murphy?" Dani asked.

"My dog," Brooke said with a huge grin. She loved Murphy. He was a playful, yet sometimes dopey black lab. Other than Rachel, he was Brooke's best friend. Unlike Rachel, he never talked back.

"You have a dog?" Davey asked excitedly.

"Yep."

"Can we meet him?" Dani asked hopefully.

"Guys, give Brooke a break," Tess implored her children.

Brooke smiled. "Sure, you can. Maybe we can bring him to get your mom's car later. I could use to change my clothes. He loves kids and he loves car rides," Brooke said. "That is if your mom says it's okay and you are up to it, D."

Tess looked at Brooke in moderate disbelief. She was beginning to think the attractive doctor was her fairy godmother. Either that or Tess was starting to worry that she had hit her head and slipped into some strange alternate reality or coma. Brooke was too good to be true. Yet, Tess felt secure in the notion that Brooke was being herself. "It's fine with me," Tess said. "But, I don't want you to feel pressured."

"About Murphy?" Brooke asked, taking a bite of her pancakes. "These are really good," she said through a mouthful.

"No, about taking me to get the car. And, don't talk with your mouthful," Tess said.

Brooke's mouth opened with her fork hanging out partially and her eyes grew wide. Both Dani and Davey started giggling at their mother's reprimand of the doctor. "She's a stickler," Dani told the doctor.

Tess started laughing and shook her head at Brooke. *Oh, God. Triple, triple trouble, Tess. Face it, you love every minute of it.*

Tess turned back to the stove and Brooke returned to eating her breakfast. *What are you doing, Campbell? This has no good place to go, none at all.* Brooke looked over at Dani who was sticking her tongue out at her brother and she smirked. She looked back up and caught Tess's gaze. *Oh, no. No. No. No. No. Brooke.* Brooke's heart fluttered perceptibly. *Friends. Keep this cool. The last thing she needs is your shit, Campbell. You want her friendship? Keep it that way.*

Tess. Tess began a mental reprimand of herself. *You barely know her. Okay, she is attractive. Oh, who am I kidding! She is more than attractive. Yes, she is nice. She seems nice. Friends. Right? That's what she said. Friends. Who are you kidding? You so want to kiss her. No, Tess. Bad idea. Very, very bad idea. You know where that will lead. Then you will lose a friend. Bad, bad, bad idea. Dani and Davey like her. Just get that out of your head.* Tess managed an uncomfortable grin. *Ignore it, Tess. It will pass. I hope.*

Brooke laughed when she opened the door to her condo and Murphy nearly knocked her over. "You fool," she chuckled, rubbing behind his ears. "Calm down, boy," she laughed harder at the panting dog. "Let me go grab a quick shower and then we will go for a ride." Murphy trotted behind his owner. Brooke made her way through the small condo and into the bathroom.

She started the shower and slipped out of her clothes from the day before, Murphy watching her every move.

"Well, Murph, I am going to take you to meet some new friends," she told the dog as she stepped into the shower. *God, I needed this.* Murphy sprawled across the navy blue bath mat that sat outside the shower. He tipped his head from side to side as Brooke regaled him with her story.

"So, Murph…We're going to go help out my friends. I think you will like them. I showed D. and Dani your picture. They're anxious to play with you, but Murph, you have to go easy on D. He thinks he's feeling better. Well, he is, but he shouldn't be running around a lot," Brooke said. She opened her eyes from underneath the hot spray of water and looked at the lab on the floor. "Listen. Murph, take it easy on him. Okay? I mean it," she warned. Murphy's tail wagged at the sound of Brooke's voice. She closed her eyes again, reached for the shampoo, and let the hot water wash over her. Her thoughts were spinning. Tess had protested more than once about Brooke coming back to help her get the car at the hospital. Brooke insisted. She felt comfortable with Tess. Tess made her laugh and Tess listened as much as she talked. Brooke had friends, but most were casual. She had Rachel, and she loved Rachel, but they kept completely opposite schedules much of the time. Between work commitments and Rachel's family, Brooke did not get to spend much time talking with her best friend. There was only one potential complication in Brooke's new friendship—attraction.

"I don't know Murph," Brooke mumbled as she shut off the shower. *I really am not sure what to do about that. Nothing, Campbell. You do nothing about it.* "Exactly!" Brooke answered the voice in her head. Murphy tipped his head in question. "Well? You weren't giving me any advice," she scolded her dog. *Which is why I love you so much, you mutt.*

Tess leaned against Brooke's car and crossed her arms over her chest. "No."

"Tess, come on. You don't seriously want to drive that car until it is cleaned. You surely do not want the kids to do a repeat Exorcist performance this afternoon. Just drive the SUV back to your house with the kids," Brooke prodded.

"No."

"Tess!"

"Brooke!" Tess was teetering between amused and annoyed. She took a deep breath. *What is it with her? Is she trying to get canonized or something?* "Brooke? Are you Catholic?"

"What?"

"Well? Are you?" Tess pushed.

"Why on earth would you ask me that?" Brooke threw her hands up.

"Because no one I know would offer to drive that car in its current condition unless they were looking to be sainted by His Holiness," Tess said flatly.

Brooke rolled her eyes and shook her head. "Tess," she said with a sigh. "I deal with disgusting things daily." Tess tipped her head in question. "Well, I do!" Brooke insisted.

Tess huffed. "I'll make you a deal," she said. Brooke waited. "I will drive my car and you drive the kids in your SUV with Murphy. God knows, they don't want to leave that dog anyway."

Brooke narrowed her gaze at Tess. She sensed that there was no way she was going to win this argument. She was quickly learning that Tess Sinclair was at least as stubborn as she was. That made Tess infinitely more interesting to Brooke. "Okay. As long as you agree to let me clean it when we get back to the house."

"What?"

"You heard me."

"Brooke, I appreciate everything you have done for us. Seriously, this is not your problem." Tess could tell that Brooke was adamant about cleaning Tess's car. She was having difficulty grasping why Brooke was so willing to go out of her way—again. She liked Brooke and the last thing she wanted to do was take advantage of the doctor's kindness. *Well, that and I don't want any expectations.* Tess sighed deeply and tried to gather her thoughts.

Brooke sensed that Tess was uncomfortable. She didn't understand why. She liked Tess. She liked Tess's kids. Tess needed some help. Not that Tess wasn't capable of handling her problems. She was. While Tess didn't complain, Brooke could see the strain on her in her demeanor at times. And, Davey and Dani were more than forthcoming with information and opinions about their mother whether Tess was present or not. The kids seemed to think Tess could use a friend. Brooke remembered the long hours her mother had endured working, taking care of a house, and dealing with all of Brooke's needs. It had never been lost on her, the strain on her mother. Brooke could help Tess. Moreover, that's what she wanted to do. The more time she spent with the affable courier and her family, the more Brooke was forced to face the fact that she needed some companionship. She needed a friend that she could both laugh with and confide in. Maybe Tess was someone who needed the same from her.

"Tess, look…I don't want to make you uncomfortable. I really," Brooke paused. "This will sound crazy."

"I doubt that," Tess said. After the last twenty-four hours, crazy seemed normal.

"I like spending time with you. I know we are just getting to know each other. Honestly, this is not something I do every day."

"No?" Tess chuckled. "Not many damsels in distress with puking kids who happen to deliver your packages that also happen to be in need of saving often, huh?"

"You do have a way with words," Brooke said. "No, there aren't, and besides you are Wonder Woman, not me. Remember?"

Tess laughed and then sighed again. She had the unshakeable feeling all day that Brooke was not going anywhere anytime soon. It took her a bit off guard. What gave her the most pause was the realization that she didn't want Brooke to go that far. "I'm not used to people helping," Tess confessed.

"Is that a superhero thing?" Brooke teased.

Tess smacked her lightly. "I wish I had that problem. Okay. You take the kids in your car. I'll meet you at my place. We'll clean the car together. Only if you let me make you dinner as a thank you."

"Deal."

It had been a long, but enjoyable day. Brooke had not been surprised to see Tess emerge from her car a bit green around the gills. She had warned her about that. While Brooke was certain she would have found the drive almost equally unpleasant, she was accustomed to tolerating offensive odors and unseemly sights. Those things came with being a doctor. She knew that Tess wanted to continue protesting Brooke's help and jump in to clean the car. It was obvious that Tess had lost her will to fight that battle after the toxic car ride home. Brooke managed to placate her friend by explaining that she would still be hungry even after the disgusting task that awaited her. Since Brooke's idea of cooking was throwing something in the microwave, it was in everyone's best interest for Tess to make dinner while Brooke took care of the car. Less reluctant than she wanted to appear, Tess had agreed.

Tess had made spaghetti for dinner. Davey had picked at picked at it and ended up having some toast and soup instead. Davey and Dani headed to bed early, exhausted from two days of upheaval. Now, Murphy was lying across Tess with his head in her lap. Brooke watched the dog close his eyes in contentment. *Big oaf. Big, lucky oaf. Don't get too used to that, you traitor.* Tess looked over and noticed that Brooke's attention had moved to one of the paintings on the wall. "That's the first one I ever painted," Tess said.

"I love it."

"Thanks. Not really that great, but I enjoy painting. It relaxes me."

"Just curious. No T.V.?" Brooke asked.

"Oh, there is. It's in the basement rec room. Just not in here. This and my bedroom are my sanctuaries. Know what I mean?" Tess said.

"I think so."

"My room?" Tess chuckled. "That sometimes doubles as the laundry staging area. So, this is my place for solitude. The kids have the rec room and their rooms. They have no issue leaving their stuff anywhere and everywhere, and I do mean *everywhere* else in this house. This is my sanity," Tess explained.

"Seems fair to me," Brooke said. She was impressed with Tess's insistence on maintaining some balance.

"Do you like the ocean?" Tess asked. It seemed that Brooke was both comfortable and curious about the beach motif in the room, particularly the paintings.

Brooke turned to her friend and reached out to scratch Murphy. "I do. I grew up near the beach."

"Here?"

"No. Until I was twelve I lived in Malibu."

"California?" Tess asked. "That Malibu?"

Brooke chuckled. "Are there others?" she asked kiddingly. Tess shrugged. "Yes," Brooke finally answered. "That Malibu."

"I always wanted to see the west coast," Tess said.

"I loved it. Still do."

"You left when your parents split?" Tess guessed.

"Yeah. Mom took the job in Connecticut. I like it there too, though. I just prefer to be closer to water," Brooke explained. "That's why I moved north a bit."

"Why not go back to California?" Tess asked curiously.

"I didn't want to be that far from my mom," Brooke answered honestly. Tess smiled. "What?" Brooke asked.

"That's sweet. What about your dad?"

"I see him a couple of times a year. That's enough for both of us," Brooke laughed. Tess looked puzzled. "Don't get me wrong, I love my dad. He's great. He was always working, even when I was there. We have a good time when we see each other. Always did. He was just busy a lot. We have lots more to talk about now."

"You mean about being doctors?"

"Yeah, there is that. And women," Brooke said with a chuckle. Tess smirked. "I just said that out loud, didn't I?"

"Sure did," Tess laughed. "But, hey, that's great. The only thing my mom wants to hear about women is that I will never date one again," she said.

Brooke grimaced. "That bad?"

"No and yes," Tess answered. Brooke looked at her to continue. Tess sighed. "Well, no, because I haven't dated anyone worth telling anyone about in three years," she said. Brooke listened intently. "Yes, because if I ever do again it will most definitely be someone of the female persuasion."

"I gather she doesn't approve?"

"Oh, I don't think she has ever quite gotten over the the daughter she thought was going to be a doctor driving a truck a truck to deliver people's packages," Tess said. "She probably probably would have been okay if I had gone to med school and married a doctor. This was not in her plan."

You still could end up with a doctor, you know. Did I just think that? Oh, Campbell. Back up lights—fast. "What about your dad?" Brooke asked.

Tess smiled broadly. "He wouldn't care if I flipped burgers. He doesn't care who I am with as long as they make me happy."

"He sounds terrific."

"He is," Tess said fondly.

"Out of curiosity," Brooke began. "What made *you* want to be a doctor? What did you think you..."

"My grandfather was a physician. A pediatrician to be exact. I loved to visit his office."

"Is that what you wanted to do? Be a pediatrician?" Brooke asked. Tess nodded a bit sadly. "Because he was one?"

"Partly," Tess sighed. "I mentioned that my brother visited last summer."

"Yeah..."

"He's two years younger than me. We had an older brother," Tess said softly. Brooke sucked in a deep breath as she listened. "He was eleven. I was nine. Leukemia. They tried everything. Everything. I remember visiting him. All those kids. Some were my age, some were older, and some were," Tess's thoughts trailed off.

"I'm sorry, Tess," Brooke reached over and took Tess's hand instinctively.

Tess looked across at her friend and smiled. She made no move to release the hand holding hers. "It was awful. It was the worst for my mom, I think. She was never the same after that. David never stopped smiling. He never complained," Tess said proudly.

Davey, David. Of course. "Sounds like he was a pretty amazing kid."

"He was," Tess said with a bright smile. "From the time I can remember I wanted to be like my grandpa. After, David…Well, I knew what I wanted to do. That never changed."

"Never?" Brooke asked gently.

"Not until the twins," Tess answered.

"Now?" Brooked wondered.

"Now? I don't know, Brooke. One thing I have learned is that you can make a difference in all kinds of ways. So, I don't know. It doesn't weigh on my mind or my heart if that's what you mean."

Brooke sensed the truth in that statement. She gently squeezed Tess's hand before letting it go. Murphy let out a half howl, half yawn. "I should get the old man here home," Brooke said.

Tess nodded. It was inevitable that their time was going to come to an end. A part of her felt unsettled by that reality. *What if this is it?* "I know, you must be tired," Tess commented.

"Not overly. I need to feed His Majesty and I do want to call Rach and check in on some things," Brooke said as she got to her feet. "Come on, Murph." Murphy picked up his head slightly, wagged his tail, and then promptly flopped back into Tess's lap and closed his eyes. Tess held back her smirk as best she could. *Really, Murph?* "Lazy ass," Brooke mumbled. "Come on, Murphy. Time to let Tess have her lap back." Murphy leisurely made his way off of Tess and strolled to his owner's side.

Tess pulled herself off of the couch and escorted Brooke Brooke to the door. She opened it slowly and watched as Murphy Murphy pounced into the front yard. "Thanks for dinner," dinner," Brooke said.

Tess shook her head at the tall doctor. She stretched and placed a kiss on Brooke's cheek. "Thank you," she whispered. Brooke blushed. *God, could you be any more adorable? Please do not let this be the last time I see you outside of work.*

"Tess?"

"Yeah?"

"Um...Would it be okay if I called? I mean...I would really like to hang out..."

Adorable. Completely. "I'd like that. So would the kids."

"So would Murphy," Brooke snickered. "I think my dog might have a crush on you." *Well, that was smooth, Brooke. Really smooth.*

"He is handsome, but he isn't really my type," Tess winked at her friend. *His owner? Oh, Tess, don't go there. She is your friend.*

Brooke cleared her throat. "So, then maybe you would give me your number? Otherwise, I will have to raid the hospital records and that is kinda frowned upon." Tess put her hand out. "What?" Brooke asked.

"Your phone?" Tess said.

"Oh!" Brooke fumbled and retrieved the phone from her pocket. She shifted a bit as Tess typed in her number. "Thanks," Brooke said.

"Text me later and then I will have yours," Tess suggested. Brooke nodded.

"I'll...Well, I'll see you...I mean, I will text you later," Brooke rambled as she walked out the door.

Tess giggled. *Adorable.* She waved as Brooke led Murphy to her SUV. *Oh, Tess, you are in some deep doo doo this time. You need a cold shower, a glass of wine, and possibly a vibrator. Did I actually just think that? Oh, no. Oh, boy. I hope I can just ignore this. What am I getting myself into?*

Tess rubbed her eyes when she heard the phone buzz on the table beside her.

Message:

Hey. It's me. Now you have my number. You are probably sleeping. If not, you should be.

Tess smiled and shook her head.

I know. Technically it is your house, your orders, but I am a doctor so you should listen to me.

Yes, Brooke, you are.

Call me whenever, Wonder Woman.

Tess thought for a moment before making a response.

If the doctor wanted me to sleep, she would have waited until morning to text me. Technically, now, it's your house, your orders. I hope Murphy has enough leg room in your bed. Just in case he makes you angry or something. Call me whenever, David Banner.

Brooke looked at her phone and smirked.

He has plenty of leg room, but Murphy thanks you for your concern. Good night, Diana.

Brooke typed in the last letters and placed the phone beside her. She grabbed hold of a pillow and pulled it to her chest. *Why do I wish I could talk to you when I just left you? So not good, Campbell. So not good.* Brooke startled when her phone buzzed.

You forgot your toothbrush. Night, Brooke.

Brooke sighed.

Tess put the phone back down and grabbed the pillow that Brooke had used the night before. A light, now familiar scent filled her senses. *Brooke. How can you miss someone you hardly know?*

Chapter Six

"I don't know!" Brooke said abruptly.

"Brooke?" Rachel called to her friend gently. Brooke's stress was palpable. Rachel had asked a simple question. Brooke had just returned to the office from the hospital. She was shaken and Rachel knew it. She also knew that Brooke would never want to admit that. Brooke put her face in her hands. "Brooke, get out of here. It's already after five. Go. Go home. Have a beer. Chill out with Murphy, I don't know. Get your mind off of it. There is nothing more you can do. It's out of your hands now."

Brooke looked up and let out a heavy breath. *Get my mind off of it? How the hell do I do that? Get my mind off what?* "I'll be fine. It goes with the territory. We both know that."

"Bullshit. I mean it, Brooke. Get out of here and catch your breath," Rachel ordered. "Don't bother arguing with me," Rachel said. She turned on her heels and headed for the door. "I don't want to see you here until Monday."

"I just had a whole weekend off," Brooke argued. "This week has been insane. I need to catch up on some things here."

"No. You need to step away. You know it and I know it. Don't make me pull rank on you, Dr. Campbell. I will."

Brooke was beginning to become angry, Technically, Rachel did have seniority. Technically, Rachel was the boss. They had never functioned that way. Rachel could be protective, but she was seldom bossy. "Fine," Brooke replied in frustration and disgust. Brooke's answer to work stress was to immerse herself in more work. Brooke's response to personal stress was to drown herself in even more work. That was not working. Rachel could see it. Brooke knew she was right, but she had no intention of admitting it. Brooke slammed her laptop shut and got up from behind her desk. She stopped in front of Rachel and looked at her harshly. "I'll see you next week."

Rachel released the nervous breath she had been holding as soon as Brooke left the office. *That went well.*

Tess opened the front door and sighed. "Come in here," she said to Brooke. Brooke's eyes were rimmed red and Tess felt her heart drop. They had traded messages on and off all week, but never saw one another. Brooke had been on the run. Tess had noted the change in the tenor of Brooke's messages gradually throughout the week. The one phone call they had shared came on Wednesday evening. It had been enjoyable. They had talked about the kids, talked about Brooke and Rachel's misadventures in medical school, and even a bit about how Tess had met Jackie. Conversation flowed smoothly between them. Neither wanted to end their chat, nor their banter, but Tess could tell that Brooke was beyond tired. She reluctantly said goodnight, hoping she would see Brooke again soon. She hadn't expected it to be so soon.

Tess closed the door. Before she had a chance to lead Brooke into the living room, Brooke broke down into tears. "Brooke," Tess said softly. She did the only thing she could and wrapped Brooke in her embrace. "Hey. What happened?"

Brooke shook from the raw onslaught of emotion. She couldn't break down in front of Rachel, not over this. Daisy Menendez was Rachel's patient. She was also someone that Rachel had come to care about on a personal level. That was a hazard in their line of work. Keeping a distance emotionally was not always possible when you interacted with someone year after year. You got to know them. You got to know their families. You saw their vulnerability and excitement. It was only human to connect. That was the case for Daisy and Rachel.

Daisy had gone into labor on Thursday. Rachel tried everything to stop it. She couldn't. Daisy fell into crisis late Thursday night. Brooke was called in. Daisy had ruptured her uterus during delivery. Brooke managed to get the baby delivered by cesarean section safely. The little girl was holding her own. Daisy, however, was struggling. Brooke had not lost many patients since going into practice with Rachel. She wasn't convinced that Daisy would pull through. The bleeding had been extensive. Brooke had managed to stop it, but Daisy had stopped breathing twice during the night and she had yet to wake up. Brooke felt horrible. Rationally, she knew that she had done everything she could. Emotionally, she found herself going over every detail again and again, wondering what she had missed. Could she have reacted faster? She was having a hard time facing Rachel. Rachel would never blame her. Brooke knew that. Somehow, Brooke couldn't seem to help blaming herself on some level.

"Brooke, talk to me," Tess implored her friend.

Brooke pulled back and looked in Tess's compassionate eyes. "I'm sorry."

"What? Sorry? Why are you sorry?"

"I show up after barely talking to you for a week and cry on your shoulder. Some greeting, huh?"

Tess pursed her lips. *Oh, no, Dr. Campbell, You are not getting out of talking that easily.* "Uh-huh. Nice try. Want to talk about it?"

Brooke couldn't help but chuckle. "Are you going to threaten me with your lasso of truth or do you need your jammies on to do that?" Brooke teased, trying to add a bit of levity. Just being with Tess made her suddenly feel lighter. And, she was not accustomed to showing her emotions so readily. Tess had that unique effect on her.

"That depends. Do I need to tie you up to get you to sit still and talk?" Tess asked.

Brooke nodded. *That might not be too far from the truth.* "Where are the kids?"

Oh, you are good, Brooke. "They're downstairs. Brooke, you don't have to tell me anything. You can tell me…"

"I know I can," Brooke said honestly. "How about ice cream first?" she suggested.

"Ice cream?" Tess questioned.

"Yeah, it cheers me up," Brooke admitted.

Too much. You are too much. "I don't think I have any ice cream," Tess said.

"So? Get the D's and we'll go get some."

"The D's?" Tess laughed. Brooke nodded. *Okay, Brooke. You win this round—ice cream first. Then I will get out a lasso if I need to. Well, duct tape might have to suffice.* Tess looked up at Brooke. *Those eyes. You would be so easy to fall for, Dr. Campbell.* "Do you want me to get them or do you want to go surprise them?" Tess asked.

Brooke brightened measurably. *She thinks they will be happy to see me.* "Up to you," Brooke tried to downplay her excitement.

Tess forced herself not to laugh. *You are not fooling me for one second, you big goof.* "Go get them. I will go get my shoes on," Tess suggested. Brooke smiled and headed off to her appointed task.

"Brooke!" Tess heard two voices yell in unison. She shook her head as she climbed the stairs. *So much trouble, Tess. You are in so, so, so much trouble.*

"So?" Tess prodded.

"What?"

"Are you trying to tell me that hot fudge cured whatever was bothering you?" Tess asked.

"No," Brooke answered honestly. "But it helps." Tess sniggered. "Thanks," Brooke said sincerely.

"For?"

"Being here helps more," Brooke admitted. *I said that. I actually just said that. Shit. It's true.*

Tess felt her heart rise dramatically. "Do you want to talk about it?"

Brooke smiled. "Yeah, I think I do."

Brooke spent the next hour telling Tess about Daisy Menendez, how the woman had so many disappointments and struggles. She told Tess how excited and happy the Menendez's were about this new baby. And then, she recapped the last forty-eight hours. Tess listened attentively and watched a myriad of emotions cross Brooke's face. There were moments when Brooke's eyes would being to water, and moments when Tess could see just a tinge of anger burning in the blue orbs that held hers. While she had never experienced what Brooke was going through, Tess was no stranger to loss and well acquainted with the feelings of helplessness and guilt. She reached across and took Brooke's hand. "You know that this is not because of you," Tess said simply.

"Rationally?" Brooke began. "Yeah, I know. I just wish that what I know would somehow change what I feel."

"I understand. All you can do is the best you have to give. That's it, and that sucks sometimes," Tess said.

Brooke smiled at her friend. *You are really something, Tess.* "It really does."

"At least you have ice cream," Tess said lightly.

"And you," Brooke said without thinking.

"And that," Tess agreed. Tess held Brooke's gaze for several minutes with neither speaking. Tess finally broke the emotional tension. "How about a movie?" Tess said. Brooke looked at her quizzically. "I'll even make popcorn. I have quite the collection downstairs. It's kind of a sickness."

"A collection of popcorn?"

Tess smacked Brooke. "Movies, you goof."

"Oh," Brooke smirked. "Romances?" she asked.

Tess hopped to her feet. "More like horror," she said as she made her way toward the kitchen.

Oh, boy. You are just full of surprises, aren't you? "What if I get scared?" Brooke called after her.

"I'll protect you," Tess called back playfully.

You just might be able to do that.

"You're in a better mood lately," Rachel observed as she took a bite from her slice of pizza.

"I am," Brooke agreed.

"Daisy is doing better," Rachel offered knowingly. Brooke nodded. "Brooke, there was nothing you could have done to change that. She's going to pull through. Not many people would have been able to get her through that," Rachel said.

"Maybe," Brooke said. "She's got a long road back."

"But, she will get back, Brooke. That's the point. She will get to be a mom, finally. You are a big part of the reason why. You are way too hard on yourself sometimes," Rachel told her friend. Brooke shrugged uncomfortably. "You've been MIA a lot lately. What have you been up to?"

"Same old," Brooke answered.

Rachel looked at her friend doubtfully. Brooke had been leaving work earlier than normal frequently the last few weeks. She also seemed more rested. Rachel had invited her over several times in the last three weeks. Brooke had declined each invitation saying she had plans. "Same old? You've had plans almost every night and all last weekend."

Brooke took a sip from her soda. "I guess."

"Who is she? Wait…let me guess…that nurse in the E.R."

Brooke laughed. "Bethany? Um, no." Rachel glared at her best friend. "There is no *her*. Not unless you mean Tess," Brooke said.

"Tess?"

"Yeah?"

"That's who all your plans have been with lately?"

"Well, only some of the time. She's teaching me to cook. She says it makes no sense that someone who is capable of using a scalpel can't use a paring knife correctly."

Rachel choked on her pizza. Brooke was learning to cook? Tess was teaching her? *What is going on here?* "I see."

"It works out for me. Murphy loves it there. He can run in the yard. It's actually got me thinking that it's time I buy a house," Brooke told her friend. This time, Rachel choked on her soda and started coughing. "You okay, Rach?"

Rachel coughed a few more times until she caught her breath. "You're buying a house?"

"When I find one. I haven't found one yet."

"Have you been looking?" Rachel asked curiously.

"Yeah. Mostly online. That's what I have been doing most nights."

"What does Tess think about that?" Rachel asked cautiously.

"About what?"

"You buying a house!"

"I don't know," Brooke shrugged and took another bite of her pizza.

"You don't know?"

"No. I haven't told her. Why? Do you think I should? Tell her, I mean," Brooke asked.

Rachel scratched her brow. *Brooke, what the hell?* "I just thought since you two were…"

"Oh, God! You think I am dating Tess!"

"Well…"

Brooke shook her head. "No. No. We're just friends," Brooke said happily.

A little too upbeat in that defense. Uh-huh. Is that what you want, Brooke? "That's good, Brooke. Tess seems like she is a great lady."

"She is," Brooke beamed. "I don't know how she does it all. Dealing with D squared every day," Brooke chuckled.

"D-squared?"

"Dani and Davey," Brooke explained.

Rachel was struggling to suppress a suspicious smile. *She doesn't even know it or does she?* "So, what are you doing this Saturday?" Rachel asked. Brooke offered her a lopsided grin. "I see. We're opening the pool. Thought maybe we would invite a few people over and barbecue."

"I'd love to, Rach. I sort of promised D. and Dani that I would do something with them," Brooke said.

Now, I have heard it all! I can barely get you to babysit Eli! "Why don't you invite Tess and her kids?" Rachel suggested casually.

"Really?"

"Sure. She's your friend, right? I'd like to get to know her past a casual hello. And, besides I think Shelia and Jamie will be there. They both have kids."

"I'll ask her," Brooke said. "She'll want to know what to bring."

Are you two married already and no one told me? She'll want to know what to bring? Do you know her blood type too? "Bring yourselves."

"That won't fly," Brooke replied. She knew Tess. The last three weeks they had not gone one day without at least a ten-minute phone conversation. Brooke was at Tess's house at least three nights a week for dinner with Murphy in tow. In some ways, Tess had become Brooke's best friend. Their relationship differed from Brooke and Rachel's. Brooke loved Rachel, but she felt a level of comfort and acceptance with Tess that she still found impossible to fathom. They just seemed to fit.

Brooke didn't censor her thoughts or feelings with Tess. Tess was open and honest. She didn't judge Brooke nor did she try to sway Brooke's feelings about life as Rachel sometimes did. The pair had traversed nearly every topic two people could delve into. Brooke felt as if she knew Tess's family. Tess had cried for hours one night recounting the last year of her brother's life. It had taken an enormous toll on the Sinclair family. Tess confessed that she often wondered what her mother would be like had David lived. Brooke had held Tess while she cried. She had felt helpless. That kind of pain and grief never truly ended. It was something that people learned to live with and navigate. It would always be seared into a person's consciousness. Brooke would have given anything to take that away from Tess. No doctor could cure that. No surgery could remove it. After a long while, Brooke suggested her favorite remedy—ice cream.

A few days later, what started as an ordinary conversation about work wound its way to Brooke confessing that she spent most of her teen years longing for her father. She had wished hat he would express pride in her. He had been disappointed at her chosen specialty when she entered medical school. It took Brooke years to recover from his reaction. He could not understand why Brooke did not pursue surgery. Surgery was a challenge and Brooke loved a challenge. She explained to Tess that she spent her childhood watching stress take its toll on her parents. More than once, she had seen her father pound a fist into the wall when he thought she was in bed. Her mother had shared some of her experiences with Brooke when Brooke was debating what specialty to pursue. The bottom line was that Brooke was sensitive and she knew it. There were times that she had to face death. That was unavoidable and each time it happened it left a small scar on her soul. Surgery was no place for Brooke, not as a way of life. She wanted to revere life. She wanted to nurture it and be nurtured by it. That was more important than a challenge. Most of the time, her career afforded her the opportunity to celebrate new possibility. That was one thing she loved about it. Tess had listened without comment. When Brooke had finished her story, Tess had smiled and kissed her on the cheek before taking Brooke's hand and leading her to the kitchen for the inevitable ice cream sundae.

Brooke looked back at Rachel. "I'll talk to Tess tonight."

Rachel smiled. *This could be very interesting.*

"Sure. The kids would love it. I mean, a pool?" Tess laughed. "What does she need me to bring?" Tess inquired. Brooke snickered. "What?"

"Oh, nothing. She said bring yourself."

"Brooke, I am not going to Dr. Cantrell's empty handed," Tess said flatly.

"It's Rachel, and I told her you would say that," Brooke replied.

"So?" Tess urged.

"I don't know! What do you want to bring? I usually pick up a six pack of something other than that crappie Coors Light Mike drinks and a bag of chips," Brooke told Tess.

"You would," Tess said.

"What's wrong with beer and chips? Real beer."

"Nothing at all," Tess assured Brooke. "Let's suppose you might bring something else this time. What might that be?"

Brooke's eyes danced. "Guacamole, chips, and good beer."

Tess leaned against the sink and shook her head. She had made guacamole one night a couple of weeks earlier for an impromptu movie night. Brooke had requested it at least a dozen times since. "You are addicted."

"I am not addicted to anything."

"I think it's that Hulk thing of yours," Tess said.

"What are you talking about, Diana?" Brooke responded in kind.

"You and green. Mint chocolate chip ice cream, guacamole, that disgusting bright green Gatorade you are so attached to. That stuff looks like it came from Fukushima. I'm surprised you don't glow in the dark—green."

"Oh, ha-ha."

"It's unnatural. This green addiction of yours," Tess continued. She loved Brooke's company. She treasured their heartfelt talks, their quiet movie nights, and their creative cooking lessons, but she loved their banter. Tess was positive that Brooke enjoyed it equally. "You know what happened to David Banner with all his genetic experimentation, you're a doctor, after all."

Brooke poked her tongue at her cheek. Tess was pleased with herself. Brooke rose slowly from her chair. "Oh, I'll give you experimentation," she wiggled her eyebrows.

"Now, Brooke," Tess held up a hand. Brooke slowly moved toward Tess, wiggling her fingers. She had discovered, not so much by accident, how ticklish Tess was. "Brooke," Tess warned sternly. Brooke's devilish smirk signaled Tess that the doctor meant business, the business of tickle torture. Tess threw the kitchen towel in her hands on the floor and took off in a sprint.

Brooke gave her about a second's head start before taking off in a deliberate stride. "I've warned you," Brooke called through the house. She turned a corner and saw Tess hiding slightly behind a floor length curtain. Brooke moved in the other direction and waited for Tess to turn her attention another way. She came up behind her. "Don't make me angry," she said grabbing hold of Tess's hips and launching into a round of light tickling.

"Stop! Brooke!" Tess was laughing so hard she could hardly breathe. She struggled to get out of Brooke's grasp and they both fell to the floor.

Brooke looked down at Tess. "You wouldn't like me when I'm angry," she said.

Tess looked up and brushed a strand of hair that had fallen out of Brooke's eyes. *Oh my God. I think I am falling in love with you.* Tess thought she was about to cry. *I am. No, this can't happen.* She looked at Brooke helplessly.

Brooke searched Tess's eyes. *You are beautiful, Tess. Brooke, stop. She is. She's gorgeous. She's...*

"Brooke?"

"Huh?"

Tess swallowed hard to regain her composure. *When did this happen? When did I go from thinking my friend was hot to love? Shit.* "If I promise to make the guacamole, will you let me up?"

Brooke sucked in a ragged breath. "Oh," she managed, still straddling her friend. *I don't really want to let you up. Let her go, Brooke. She's your friend. That is for the best and you know it.* "You'll make my guac?"

Tess arched her eyebrow. "*Your* guac?" *Oh, God. I wish you would just kiss me. Bad idea, Tess. Don't screw up the best thing you've had in a long time. She's your friend.*

"Yes, *my* guac. Well? Will you?" Brooke responded with another threat of tickling.

"I give. I'll even pick you up some of that nuclear Gatorade you love," Tess said. *Just please, please, let me up before I do something I will regret.*

Brooke pretended to consider the request thoughtfully. "Okay," she finally said as she hopped to her feet. "Extra garlic and no onions."

Tess accepted Brooke's hand and let Brooke pull her up. "Fine by me since you are doing all the chopping."

"What?"

"Got to practice those knife skills sometime," Tess deadpanned.

She always wins. No matter what, she always ends up on top. Brooke shook her head. *Well, almost always.*

Chapter Seven

"Brooke!" Davey yelled. Brooke turned her attention to the far end of the pool. "Watch!" he called back.

"I'm watching!" Brooke called over. Davey stepped back a few paces to get a running start and flew into the pool in his best cannonball position. Brooke laughed as he surfaced triumphantly. "Nice form, D.!" Davey gave her the thumbs up before swimming to the edge, pulling himself up, and getting ready for a repeat performance.

"They're having fun," a perky blonde commented.

"Yeah. Murphy was their favorite thing until they met Rachel's pool," Brooke admitted with a chuckle.

"How are you, Brooke?" Sheila asked.

"I'm good. How have you been, Sheila? Looks like Jack is having fun with D. and Dani," Brooke commented.

"He is, I think. It's nice for him to have someone his own age to play with," Sheila said.

"It's good for them too. I mean, they have each other. Sometimes that's a really good thing and sometimes," Brooke trailed off with a shake of her head. Dani and Davey blew hot and cold. Some days Brooke considered the possibility that they were actually Siamese Twins they were so in sync. Other times, they seemed total opposites. D. would torment Dani by any and all means possible until Dani reached her breaking point. When it managed to get that far, it was ugly. Sometimes, it became physically ugly. The week before, one of their wrestling matches had resulted in a broken end table. Brooke had thought for a moment by the popping veins in Tess's neck that she might be required to perform surgery. The table she could fix. If Tess got hold of the twins, Brooke was not so sure she would be able to repair the damage. She snickered at the memory.

"Tess seems great," Sheila said.

"Tess? She's the greatest," Brooke said sincerely. *The greatest mom. The greatest cook. The greatest at Angry Birds. The greatest friend. The greatest...*

"Never thought I would see the day, I have to say," Sheila said as she looked across the patio to where Tess and Rachel were engaged in a conversation.

"What day?"

"Oh, come on, Brooke. I never pegged you for settling down."

"What are you talking about?"

Sheila looked at Tess and then back to Brooke. *Is she seriously telling me they are not together?*

"The kids seem to be having a good time," Rachel said to Tess.

"Davey is a fish. I swear, there are times I wonder if he is part dolphin."

Rachel laughed. She had been talking with Tess for nearly half an hour and the conversation had yet to dwindle. *I can understand what she sees in you, that's for sure.* "Mike is determined to get Eli into swimming. He likes his bath better, I think," Rachel pointed to her husband and son.

"It's the temperature. Dani is like that too. Heated pool and she will not leave. Cold water? She dips in each toe for twenty minutes. By the time she's up to her knees, it's time to go and she is pitching a fit," Tess laughed.

"Different kids, huh?"

"In some ways, completely. In others, I would think they were clones not twins."

"I can't imagine twins," Rachel said with an exasperated breath. "Every time I deliver multiples, I thank God I only got one. And, I pray it is one at a time," she admitted.

Tess watched her son maneuvering closer to her daughter. Dani was standing near the edge of the pool, still mostly dry. Tess had a feeling that was going to change soon. She smiled at Rachel. "At first, I was scared shitless," Tess admitted. "God, I was barely ready for one at twenty-one, much less two," she said. Rachel nodded. "But, I wouldn't have it any other way. I suppose it's like anything else."

"What do you mean?" Rachel asked.

"Well, I mean that some things you just don't get a choice in. You don't choose to be born. You don't get to choose when to die or who lives and dies. You don't even get to choose who you fall in love with," Tess said softly. "Same with kids. You can choose to have them, but you don't get to choose who they are. In my case, I didn't choose twins. That's just what I was given. You take the ups with the downs and the good with the bad. I guess that's how I see it. I was terrified when they were born, but mostly of losing them or hurting them. They're the best thing that ever happened to me, and as much as they drive me insane at times, they would be as lost without each other as I would be without them," Tess explained.

Smart lady. Wow, Brooke, I hope you realize how lucky you are. Rachel caught a glimpse of Sheila talking to Brooke. Sheila was an anesthesiologist who had been eyeing Brooke for a few years. In fact, there were quite a few women hoping to catch Brooke's eye. Rachel adored Sheila. She had thought that Sheila had given up that ghost. She also would have thought that the beautiful blonde would have surmised that Brooke was taken. *Which you are, Brooke. Whether you want to admit it or not, you are very, very taken.* Rachel had no intention of taking any chances.

"Let's go see what our favorite doctor is doing," Rachel suggested. "I don't trust her not to eat all that guacamole you brought by herself. She's been grazing all day," Rachel whispered to Tess. Tess laughed. She had a terrific time chatting with Rachel, but she was ready to get back to Brooke.

"She has a problem with green things," Tess said. Rachel looked at Tess curiously. "I'll explain later," Tess promised.

"What are you talking about?" Brooke asked Sheila.

"I just assumed you two were together," Sheila said.

"Me and Tess?"

"Uh, yeah."

"Why does everyone think that?" Brooke asked pointedly. *Maybe because you can't keep your eyes off of her, Brooke. Stupid. She doesn't see you that way. You need to get over this. She is the best friend you have now, maybe ever.* "We're friends, that's all."

Sheila considered the statement for a moment. "So? Is she straight?"

Brooke sprayed some of the beer she was sipping out. *Are you interested in Tess, Sheila? What the hell kind of question is that?*

"Guess that answers that question."

"Sheila, it's not my place…"

"You said she is great. Look, Brooke, I don't want to step on any toes here," Shelia said.

Rachel and Tess were strolling over to Brooke's location when Tess suddenly stopped.

"Sheila, if you are interested in Tess…"

"I don't want to…"

"Tess deserves someone nice," Brooke said. *Yeah, Brooke, that's right, she does. Be a big girl and do the right thing here.* "She's not my girlfriend. You should talk to her. She's..."

"Great, I know," Sheila said. "Thanks."

Tess's stomach lurched so violently that thought she was about to be sick. "Tess," Rachel took hold of Tess's arm. "Hey…"

"I need to use the bathroom," Tess said. "Sorry. Excuse me."

Sheila smiled at Rachel and walked back toward the pool as Tess headed into the house. Brooke saw Tess opening the sliding glass doors. Her hand had moved to her eyes. "Rach? Is Tess okay?" Brooke asked in concern.

Rachel glared at her best friend. *You may well be the most stupid person I know!* Rachel shrugged.

"Rach? What's going on?"

"You know what, Brooke?" Rachel answered with her own question. Brooke was taken off guard. "That is an excellent question. Maybe you should figure that out," Rachel shook her head in disgust and walked away.

"What?" Brooke called after her. *Why is she pissed? What the hell? First Sheila. Now Rachel. Something is up with Tess. What did I do to deserve this?*

Brooke waited a while to see if Tess would emerge. She wasn't sure how much time had passed, but it was enough that she was beginning to get nervous. She was just about to ask Rachel to keep an eye on the kids when Tess began to approach. Brooke started to move, but she felt as if everything were in slow motion. *Something is wrong. I can feel it.*

Tess had spent the better part of a half-hour in the bathroom. For a few minutes, she truly thought she was going to be physically ill. Reality had hit her hard and unexpectedly. The fact that she had fallen in love with Brooke was bad enough to finally accept. Tess had sworn off relationships. That is what made it so strange that Brooke's words to Sheila felt like such a knife in the heart. *She doesn't love you that way, Tess. Accept it. Move on. Brooke is your friend. You have no right to be angry or even hurt. You're friends. She can't help what she doesn't feel. What did you expect? A successful, beautiful woman to take on a working class, single mom, and her two kids? Grow up, Tess. Be an adult and let it go or you'll lose her friendship.*

"Tess?" Brooke finally reached her friend. *Oh no, she was crying.* "Hey, what's going on?"

Tess smiled weakly. Her tears were surfacing again and the last thing she wanted was for Brooke to know the reason why. "Just not feeling too well," Tess said.

Bullshit, Tess. What is going on? Did someone say something to you? I'll kill them. "Tess?"

"Really," Tess promised. "I'm just feeling a little funny."

"Do you want to leave?" Brooke asked. "I'll take you home right now. We can just watch a movie. We don't have to stay…"

Tess grasped Brooke's hand. *She does love you, Tess, just not the way you love her. Take it for what it is. She's the best thing you have going besides those kids.* This time, Tess smiled more genuinely. "No. I'll be okay. I just need to sit for a bit, I think."

Brooke nodded. She sensed there was something Tess was not telling her. Something told her not to push. "Okay. You want me to get you something?" Brooke asked.

Tess shook her head. *The only thing I want right now, I can't have.* "No. I'm okay. I promise. Go visit with your friends. I'm going to go watch the kids for a bit."

Brooke helplessly watched Tess walk away. *What aren't you telling me?*

Brooke knocked on Tess's front door and waited. They had spoken every day as they always did, but Brooke sensed the distance between them. She was hoping that was either in her sometimes overactive imagination, or the result of fatigue from being on call. One thing, Brooke did know, she did not want to go on wondering. Brooke was due to head down to Connecticut to spend the weekend with her mother. She'd been considering postponing the trip all week. It was only three days. Right now, for some reason beyond her rational explanation, Brooke had a nagging feeling three days was too long.

Tess took a deep breath and opened the door. She was determined that things would resume as they had always been. That was proving more difficult than Tess could have imagined. She had tried over the past days to place when she had fallen for her friend. Attraction had always been present, but love? That was Tess's problem currently. She couldn't place it. To Tess, it felt almost as if she had always loved Brooke. She'd tossed and turned each night, replaying the last month of her life. More than a few times, Tess had heard it said that people fall in love in an instant. That had never been the way for Tess. She had liked Jackie. She had liked Daniel. She felt attraction, even passion. Perhaps she had grown to love them, it certainly had not happened in an instant.

Her worst moment had come on Monday night. She opened the freezer to take something out for dinner the next day and came face to face with a half-gallon of mint chocolate chip ice cream. She laughed through the sobs that racked her body over the absurdity of the situation. She was crying over ice cream. Not just ice cream, Brooke's ice cream. When had she started adding Brooke's favorite things to her grocery list? Tess couldn't remember. When had she not kept mint chocolate chip ice cream? When had she not stocked the refrigerator with disgusting green Gatorade? She laughed and sobbed, and repeated the cycle for what seemed like hours. Logically. Tess knew that these were new evolutions in her life. Emotionally, it felt as if Brooke had always been here, even when she wasn't.

Now, she had to face the friend she had unwittingly fallen deeply in love with. *Maybe love was just not meant for me.* The thought had passed through Tess's mind numerous times since Saturday night. The worst part of all of it was that Tess seemed sure she would never love anyone the way she loved Brooke

Campbell. She never had before. In some ways, it reminded her of losing her brother. He had been her best friend. David was a part of her in a way that she could never hope to explain. She told him her secrets. He made her laugh. He drove her crazy. She had loved him beyond measure. She would miss him for the rest of her life. Brooke was still here. Still, Tess understood that she would miss Brooke too on some level. It brought an odd emptiness to her soul. At the same time, Tess had never felt her heart so full. It was confusing. She needed to let go and accept Brooke's friendship as it had always been. She was determined to do just that.

Tess opened the door slowly. "Hi."

Brooke smiled. "Hey."

"You ready for some cooking and some scream queens?" Tess asked with a smile. *God, I missed you, Brooke. This is so hard. I wish you knew how hard this is.*

"Make me your victim," Brooke joked. *Tess, please tell me what is bothering you.*

Preparing dinner seemed to chip through the wall that had somehow been erected between them. Brooke's struggles to follow directions sometimes drove Tess to distraction. It was also incredibly amusing. Tess loved to watch Brooke chopping vegetables and measuring spices. She understood perfectly that Brooke was capable of becoming a master chef if she had the inclination. She suspected that much of Brooke's helplessness in the kitchen was playfully deliberate. The other part was some crazy mental block that Brooke had built in her mind that she had no domestic abilities whatsoever. Moving about the kitchen with the twins making their presence known, threw the pair into a familiar pace and routine. Little by little, Tess forgot to think. Brooke was with her. They were in sync. For the time, that was all that seemed to matter.

Brooke felt a sense of relief when she and Tess finally sat down to watch a movie. She watched as Tess began to nod off.

You haven't been sleeping. Me neither. Tess's eyes finally fell shut and her head began to drop. Brooke put her arm around Tess and let Tess's head fall on her shoulder. She closed her eyes, the noises from the television fading like lights in the distance. The woman now in her arms calmed her. Brooke kissed Tess's head gently. *I should stay home. I promised Mom. Why do I feel like I need to stay home?* Brooke felt Tess move closer to her. "It's okay. Sleep," Brooke whispered.

"Miss you," Tess mumbled.

Brooke was puzzled. *Who do you miss? Tess, what is going on in your head? Why won't you tell me? You tell me everything.* Brooke sighed and held Tess a bit tighter. *What am I doing?*

Tess woke up and decided to stay exactly where she was a while longer. It was selfish, but being in Brooke's arms felt safe. She wasn't sure she would ever experience that again, and if that was selfish, she didn't care. She fought to contain the tears that began to fill her eyes. *Shit. Don't, Tess. Get up. Just get up. You can't do this. It's not fair to either of you.* Tess forced herself out from under Brooke's grasp. Brooke groaned and Tess couldn't help but giggle at the perturbed expression on Brooke's sleeping face. *Adorable.* Tess gingerly guided Brooke back onto the couch and covered her with a blanket. She watched Brooke sleep for a few minutes, memorizing her features. Slowly she bent over and placed a kiss on Brooke's forehead. "I love you, Brooke," she admitted before making her way from the room.

Chapter Eight

"Brooke?" Rebecca Sinclair called to her daughter. Brooke looked up. Rebecca sighed and then smiled. "All right, let's have it."

"Huh?"

"You've been brooding all day long."

"I am not brooding," Brooke chuckled. "I just have a lot on my mind."

"Work?" Rebecca asked.

"No," Brooke admitted. "I'm thinking of buying a house," she said. Brooke's mother's eyes expressed her surprise. "Why does everyone I tell look at me like I've lost my mind."

"It's just not something that you have ever talked about before," her mother pointed out.

"Things change."

Rebecca smiled. "Yes, they do. So, what has changed?" Brooke shifted nervously in her chair. "Brooke?"

"I just think it's time. Murphy needs space. You've seen him! Plus, what if I wanted to have guests or something like that? My condo is too small. There's no place for kids to run or people to sleep."

"Kids to run?" Rebecca questioned. "Worried about Eli when he gets older?" Brooke shrugged. "Brooke, is this about Tess?"

Brooke shifted again. She had told her mother a great deal about Tess and the twins. Most of her free time was spent with the threesome. She'd answered the phone one Thursday night from Davey's baseball practice. That led to questions. That led Brooke to the story of how she and Tess ended up friends because of a mishap with pizza and then Davey's midnight appearance in the emergency room. She had not shared her feelings with anyone, and certainly not her mother. If she didn't intend to tell Tess how she felt, she was not going to tell anyone else either. Romantic relationships were a bad idea. She had convinced herself of that a long time ago. So, why was she suddenly determined to buy a house? Brooke sighed outwardly. It was about Tess and she knew it. She wanted a place that Tess and the kids could enjoy. Brooke was always at Tess's house. No matter how much she tried to give, it seemed to Brooke as if Tess was always taking care of her too. She cooked for Brooke. She kept the things Brooke liked to eat in the house. She'd even done Brooke's laundry a few times. She had taken over babysitting Murphy when Brooke was on call. Tess took care of everything. She deserved an escape too. Brooke wanted to be able to have Tess over and take care of Tess. Maybe she could get a place with a pool. The kids would love that.

"Brooke?"

"Mom, Tess is…" Rebecca grinned knowingly. "She's my best friend. Not like Rachel, it's different," Brooke tried to explain. Rebecca nodded. "It's just…it's different. I can't explain it."

"Different in a way that makes you feel compelled to buy a house," Rebecca pointed out casually.

"We are always at her place. Murphy practically lives there with my schedule," Brooke said. Rebecca snickered. "What?"

"You're in love."

"What?"

"Well? Aren't you?" Rebecca started to laugh harder at her daughter's wide-eyed expression. "Good Lord, Bee. You look like a deer caught in the headlights. It happens."

"Not to me," Brooke mumbled.

"And why would that be?" Rebecca asked. Brooke grew pensive. "Bee?"

"You haven't called me Bee in a long time."

"You didn't answer me. What makes you think that love can't happen for you?"

"Mom, my life is not made for relationships," Brooke said flatly.

"Seems to me that you are already in a relationship, Bee."

"A friendship. Not the same."

"Oh? Why is that? Because you are not sleeping with her?" Rebecca asked.

"Exactly."

"I hate to burst your bubble, Bee. I have known plenty of married couples who didn't sleep together."

"Unhappily married, I am sure," Brooke quipped.

"Are you unhappy?"

"I'm not married," Brooke reminded her mother.

"But, you are in love. So, what? You aren't attracted to Tess?" Rebecca asked.

"Mom!"

"Well?" Rebecca pushed. Brooke groaned. "That's what I thought. Now, what is this all about?"

"What do you mean?"

"What are you talking about that your life is not made for a relationship?"

Rebecca wanted to hear Brooke's answer. She waited patiently. Brooke was agitated. She had struck a nerve. Sometimes dealing with Brooke reminded Rebecca a great deal of performing surgery. There were pieces, fragments of Brooke that could become scattered. It took time to discern them and then move them back into place. Rebecca had chalked up Brooke's lack of long-term relationships for many years to the fact that Brooke was trying to establish her career. That time had passed. There was not one question in her mind that Brooke was in love. Every time Brooke called in the last month, the main topic had been Tess, D., and Dani. Rebecca felt as if she already knew them. Brooke's voice had a noticeable lilt. Rebecca didn't need to meet Tess to understand the impact she had made on Brooke's life and her heart. Rebecca could not understand why Brooke seemed determined to resist her own happiness.

"Brooke!" Rebecca demanded an answer.

"It's a bad idea. If anyone should know that, it should be you," Brooke said a bit angrily.

"Me? What are you talking about?"

"Being a doctor. Too much division. I made my choice when I chose medicine. I debated that in college. What did I want? A family or medicine? I made my choice."

"Oh, Brooke," Rebecca closed her eyes. She felt as if the world had crashed down on her.

"I'm not doing that to Tess. She's had enough things she had to give up already. I can be there as her friend. I won't disappoint her that way. She already had to give up her aspirations, just like you did."

Rebecca looked at her daughter in astonishment. "Like I did? Brooke, what on earth are you talking about?"

"I watched you. You left because dad was never there. I always understood that. You gave up everything. Gave up your career, came here…for me. And why? Because it was medicine or me. You always said that I am like him. I am. Right? Like Dad?"

Rebecca folded her hands in front of her face and tried to steady her emotions. In a heartbeat, Brooke had transformed into a wounded child. *Where did you get these ideas, Bee?* She took a deep breath and moved to kneel before her daughter. *It's time we had a talk, Bee.*

Tears of frustration had begun to stream down Brooke's cheeks. Rebecca took her daughter's hands and spoke softly. "I'm so sorry, Bee. You are very much like your father," she said gently. Brooke looked up at her mother, sadness painting her eyes. Rebecca wiped her daughter's tears away. "That's not a bad thing, Bee. Your father is not just an excellent surgeon. He is a good man."

"That doesn't change…"

"No, it doesn't. The challenge for him was everything. He loves you as much as I love you. He just shows it differently."

"He didn't love you enough," Brooke said quietly.

Rebecca smiled. "No, Bee…You are wrong. He still loves me. I still love him." Brooke looked at her mother doubtfully. "Why does that surprise you?"

"That's even worse," Brooke mumbled.

"No. We parted friends. We changed. That's all. It happens, Bee. Life doesn't give you guarantees. Some things you just can't control and you just can't change. You do the best you can with the hand you are dealt. You make the choices you need to so you can be happy. That's all anyone can do, just they best they can."

"You gave everything up," Brooke said. "Tess already did that once."

"I gave nothing up," Rebecca said assuredly. "I had you. That was everything. For me, it still is."

"Mom, you could have been…"

"I have been exactly what I wanted to be, Bee. I love what I do. I love teaching. I don't love it more than I love you. I don't love anything more than that. You have some idea that I quit the operating room because of you. That's not true," she said. Brooke looked back at her mother hopefully. "I did love that part of my life. But, Bee, I have told you before, it took a toll on me. Sometimes, I made a real difference. Sometimes….it was just too much. Pieces. I got tired of seeing people in pieces, Bee. One day, about a year before your father and I split up, they brought a young boy into the emergency room. Pieces. There were so many pieces, one of the residents called him Humpty Dumpty. He woke up for a few minutes and I looked into his eyes. Maybe, maybe I could put his leg back together. Maybe his knee. I could never put the pieces of his soul that were shattered. Both his parents were gone. Head on collision. He was ten. I couldn't do that anymore. I could teach people how. That's the best I could do. What if that had been you, Bee? That's all I could see for weeks? What if it had been your father and me? Life is unpredictable. All that really matters are the people you love."

"Mom..."

"You have always understood that, Bee. That's why you made the choice to do what you do. What did you tell me? You wanted to revere life more than you wanted to repair it. There is no greater part of life than love, sweetheart. Not one. If you want to revere life, you have to love. That means you have to risk."

Brooke shook her head. "I don't know how."

"Yes, you do. You are already doing it."

Brooke looked up fearfully. "What if I hurt her?"

Rebecca kissed her daughter's cheek. "You will," she said. Brooke swallowed hard. "And, at some point she will hurt you. If you are lucky, and you really love each other, you will get through those moments."

"You didn't."

"No. But, I am not Tess and you are not your father. Don't make us your barometer, Bee. But, if it helps, neither of us have any regrets, not about each other and not about you. Your father would tell you the same thing. I guarantee it."

"I don't even know what..."

"Call Tess, Bee. Just call her."

"I'm glad you had some time," Sheila said.

Tess smiled at the other woman. She had found Sheila's company pleasant. It had been a welcome distraction. Tess was still reeling. That was made worse by the fact that she missed Brooke. Brooke had sent her a message when she arrived at her mother's home. They hadn't spoken since. Tess had hesitated briefly to accept Sheila's invitation to get their kids together. Davey and Dani had been talking about Sheila's son Jack all week long. In the end, Tess rationalized that this was a necessary evolution. The kids were running through Tess's backyard chasing Murphy. *Brooke.* Brooke was always present even when she was far away.

"They certainly have a lot of energy," Sheila laughed.

"That they do," Tess agreed just as her phone rang. "Sorry," she said to Sheila. "Hey."

"Hi," Brooke said.

"Everything okay?" Tess asked.

"Jack! Don't push the dog!" Sheila yelled across the yard.

"Bad time?" Brooke asked.

"No. Sheila just brought Jack over to play with the kids," Tess said. Silence lingered. "Brooke?"

"I'm sorry. I didn't know you had plans."

Tess detected something strange in Brooke's voice. "It's okay. Are you okay?"

"Yeah, yeah, of course. Listen, I'm sorry I bothered you."

"You didn't."

"I should let you go. Tell the kids I said hello," Brooke choked back her tears.

"I will. Brooke? Are you sure everything is okay there?" Tess asked.

Brooke took a deep breath and remained determined not to let Tess hear her sadness. "Absolutely. I'll see you Monday when I pick up Murph."

Tess frowned. "Okay. Have fun with your mom."

"Yeah. Say hi to Sheila."

"Sure. See you Monday," Tess said. She was fairly certain Brooke had hung up before she had a chance to finish the thought.

"Everything okay?" Sheila asked.

Tess looked at her phone. "I don't know."

Rebecca waited nearly an hour before searching out Brooke. She wanted to give her time to talk to Tess, but the eerie quiet from Brooke's room was beginning to unnerve her. She did not expect to find Brooke on her bed crying. "Bee?"

"It's my fault."

"What happened? Did you and Tess have a fight or something?"

"No," Brooke chuckled through her tears. "She has *company*."

"What kind of company?"

"Sheila kind of company," Brooke groaned. "And Jack."

"Jack?"

"Sheila's son."

Rebecca pursed her lips. "I see. And, that is a bad thing?"

"Not for Sheila," Brooke said sarcastically.

"What about for Tess?" Rebecca asked.

"What do you mean?" Brooke sighed dramatically. "I told her that if she was interested she should try to get to know her. Well, guess she listened."

"Tess?"

"No! Sheila!"

"So, Sheila is interested in Tess. Is that what you think?" Rebecca tried to regain her footing.

"Of course, she is! Tess is beautiful. Plus she's funny as hell and is a great mom. She's great! Just like I told Sheila," Brooke said. "Fuck me."

Rebecca forced herself not to laugh. "So? Why are you here?"

"What?"

"Well, if Sheila wants Tess and you want Tess, and Sheila is there....Why are you here?"

"Mom!"

"Brooke!"

"I don't even know how she feels."

"Well, there is only one way to find that out, and it certainly is not here."

"Mom, I can't just drive to Tess's, knock on the door and say, 'Hi. Sorry to drop in but I thought you should know that I am in love with you.'" Rebecca smiled broadly. "What?" Brooke asked.

"Is that the first time you said it out loud?" Rebecca asked. Brooke grinned in spite of herself. "Feels good to admit it, doesn't it?" Rebecca asked knowingly. "I'm not suggesting that you drive home and ask her to move into this house you want to buy and marry you. I do think what you just said is perfect."

"Just knock on the door and tell her I love her?" Brooke asked in disbelief.

"Pretty much, yes."

"I'm calling Dad."

"Why?"

"You need a trauma surgeon. You must have fallen and hit your head," Brooke said.

"Very funny, Bee. Say whatever you want. Just tell her."

"What if she laughs at me?" Brooke asked.

"The woman who has managed to get you to attempt cooking, who babysits your dog for days at a time? The same woman whose children you have been taking to rehearsals and practices? That woman? Somehow, Brooke, I think it might be you who needs the trauma surgeon. You are clearly missing something here."

"What is that supposed to mean?" Brooke asked.

"Bee, you are going to have to make a choice. What do you want?"

Brooke whispered her answer. "I want Tess."

Rebecca grabbed the duffel bag Brooke had brought and tossed it at her. "Call me tomorrow."

"What?" Brooke said.

"I am still the parent, and I am kicking you out. At least for this weekend." Brooke was stunned. "Well?" Rebecca asked. "It's just about five. Leave now, and you will be there by the time she is putting those kids to bed. And, I will bet your nemesis will be gone by then."

"You don't know that," Brooke said.

"No, but I will bet you a weekend at the Vineyard that I am right. In fact, I will bet you a weekend at the Vineyard with Tess, and I will even babysit."

Brooke laughed. Her mother could always cajole her out of an emotional funk. "You don't even know what she'll say."

"Didn't bet on that," Rebecca pointed out. "I just bet that her friend would be gone when you got there. Either way, if I'm right, you win and get a trip to the Vineyard. So?"

Brooke seldom backed down from a challenge and her mother was issuing her one right now. "Fine. You are on."

"Good. Call me tomorrow and let me know when I should book you a room."

"I'll do that, oh confident one," Brooke said. She grabbed her duffel bag and marched out of the room.

Rebecca flopped onto Brooke's bed. *Works like a charm every time.*

It had been a full day of activity. Tess was ready for some quiet time. Sheila had helped a sleepy Jack into her car and was now standing on Tess's front step. "Thanks for today," Sheila said.

Tess smiled at her. Tess had to admit that it was refreshing in its own way to know that someone was attracted to her. It was even a bit tempting. Sheila was funny. She was charming and intelligent. And, she was definitely not hard to look at. Slightly taller than Tess, Sheila had bluish-green eyes and blonde hair that was the color of champagne. Tess thought that

Sheila looked a great deal more like a doctor that you would see on a television medical drama than one that you expected to actually knock you out. In other words, Sheila was a knockout. *Ironic.*

"Thanks for coming over. The kids had a great time," Tess said. "So did I," she added. That was the truth. Tess appreciated the company. It had taken her focus off of her aching heart for a few hours. She had laughed more than she had expected to. Sheila had some hysterical stories and a knack for telling them.

A smiling Tess was caught by surprise when the woman in front of her leaned closer. "I'm glad," Sheila said softly. Before Tess could complete a thought, Sheila's lips were on hers.

Tess closed her eyes instinctively. It had been longer than she cared to admit since she had felt the softness of another person's lips on her own. Her heart fluttered slightly at the contact, and then swiftly plummeted. Tess gently pushed Sheila back. "I can't," she whispered regretfully. *I wish I could. I can't.*

Sheila looked at Tess and smiled sadly. "Tess," Tess opened her eyes and smiled, but her eyes were glistening with tears. "Why not?" Sheila asked softly.

"I'm in love with someone else," Tess replied honestly.

"Brooke," Sheila hung her head and barely whispered. She looked back at Tess. "Tess, Brooke has never been…"

"I know," Tess said. "It doesn't matter. It doesn't change anything." *No, it really doesn't. Face it, you don't want anyone else.*

Sheila nodded. "I hope we can still be friends," she said.

Tess heard hopefulness and sadness mingling in Sheila's voice. "I'd like that."

"I'm sorry," Sheila said. "For what it's worth, I think she is crazy." Tess let out the hint of a chuckle at the sentiment. "I'll see you."

"I hope so," Tess said honestly. She waited until Sheila climbed into her car and closed the front door. Unexpectedly, a wave of emotion sent Tess sliding down her door until she hit the floor. She covered her face with her hands and let the heartbreak consume her. *Love is not supposed to hurt so much. Why does it always have to hurt so much?* Murphy sheepishly approached her and began licking the hands covering her face. Tess laughed as she cried. "What am I going to do, Murph?"

Brooke turned onto Tess's street and fought an onslaught of severe nausea. "No turning back, Brooke," she ordered herself. She pulled in front of the small house and turned off the car. The living room light was on. Sheila's car was nowhere. "Guess, I will be going to the Vineyard," she said. *The question is, will I be alone? Are you sure about this, Brooke? What are you going to say when she laughs at you? What if she doesn't? Everything will change. You ready for that, doc?* Brooke took a deep breath and closed her eyes tightly. "I don't know," she confessed. *Yes, you do.* Brooke opened her eyes, stepped out of the car and looked at the house a few yards away. She stood there for a few minutes, thoughts swirling. Brooke suddenly heard her mother's voice echoing in her brain. *All that really matters are the people you love.* With a shake of her head and another deep breath, Brooke headed for Tess's front door.

Tess thought she heard a car. She had cried for what seemed like hours. She wasn't sure how long it had been. Davey had walked in and she was forced to compose herself. As soon as the twins were in bed, she found herself on the couch sobbing into Murphy's back. The big lab brought her a small measure of comfort. His love was unconditional. At that moment, his sloppy affection was welcome. Not what she wanted, but a comfort that she needed. She sat up curiously when a knock fell on the front door. “What the hell?” she muttered. Tess headed for the door and peeked out the window. “Brooke?”

Brooke was positive that she was going to faint. She could feel the blood swishing through her veins. Her heart was racing so swiftly that she could hear it in her ears. The door opened. There she was—Tess. They stared at each other for a moment. Brooke immediately took note of the puffiness in Tess’s eyes. Tess’s tears began to fall swiftly against her will. Brooke reached out and took Tess’s face in her hands. She seemed to lose all hope of rational thought in one instant. Tess did not need to answer any questions. She didn’t need to say a word. The truth was written in her eyes. Brooke pulled her close and held her while she cried.

Tess fell into Brooke. The strength and tenderness she found in Brooke’s embrace availed itself in more tears. Brooke closed her eyes and held the woman she loved. *Say it, you idiot.* “I love you, Tess,” she whispered as tears began to fill her eyes.

Tess’s heart skipped several beats. She pulled back slightly and looked at Brooke. Brooke’s lopsided grin revealed her insecurity. Tess stroked Brooke’s cheek. She found herself speechless. *Did you just say that you love me?* “Did you just tell me that you love me?” she asked.

“Yes, I did,” Brooke said nervously. They were words she had never spoken. She had never wanted to and she had never expected to. Tess was lost in an endless search of Brooke’s eyes. “Tess?”

Tess was awestruck. She reached up and held Brooke’s face in her hands. She was helpless to speak. Brooke needed an answer. Tess pulled Brooke’s head down gently and brought their lips together. Brooke met her so gently that Tess sighed. She sensed a brewing passion lying in wait beneath the surface. At this moment, what passed between them was a long-awaited confession.

"I love you too," Tess said as she released Brooke slowly from their kiss.

Brooke smiled and tucked Tess's hair behind her ears. "Can I come in now?" she asked.

Tess chuckled. She took Brooke's hand and led her through the door. *Now, what?*

Tess was lying with her head in Brooke's lap. Murphy had collapsed at Brooke's feet. "I'm sorry," Brooke said.

"No. It doesn't matter," Tess said.

Tess had just finished explaining to Brooke that she had overheard Brooke and Sheila talking. Rachel's recent standoffish attitude and the distance that Brooke sensed between her and Tess suddenly made sense. *You really can be a jerk.* "Yes, it does matter," Brooke said. Tess sighed. "Tess, you are the last person I ever want to hurt."

Tess smiled. "She kissed me," she said.

Brooke felt ill. "Sheila?" she asked. Tess lifted her eyebrow with a guilty grin. "I, I…what…" Brooke stammered.

"I told her I was in love with someone else," Tess said. She watched as Brooke's insecurity shifted into recognition.

"Was she mad?" Brooke wondered.

"No. Disappointed, I think," Tess said. "What made you come home?"

"Mom," Brooke answered. "She sort of set me straight." Tess's eyes sparkled with curiosity. Brooke sighed. "Tess, I won't lie to you. This scares the shit out of me."

"I know it does. It scares me too."

Brooke nodded. "But, I swear to you, I've never wanted anything more in my life," Brooke said. Tess was surprised. "I'm serious," Brooke continued. "I don't know what the hell I am doing. I've never had a real relationship. I swore I never would."

"What changed?" Tess asked.

"You. I can't…I don't want to be without you, and I don't mean just as my friend. I know what that means, at least, I think I do."

"It isn't just me," Tess said apprehensively.

"Yes, I know," Brooke smiled. She had no illusions about what loving Tess meant. It meant a ready-made family. She was a bit shocked that as frightening as the implications of that were, Brooke found the possibility of losing Tess and her family far more terrifying.

Tess smiled up at Brooke. "One day at a time," she said. "I want this to work."

"One day at a time," Brooke agreed. Tess accepted Brooke's kiss gratefully. She caressed Brooke's neck and pulled her closer. Brooke's tongue brushed over hers and Tess felt a deep ache surface slowly from the connection. She had to concentrate on breathing when Brooke pulled back. "So," Brooke began. Tess looked at her curiously. "In the interest of one day at a time, could I maybe start the next one with you waking up beside me?"

Tess smiled. She understood the proposition for what it was. "You just want to use that toothbrush again," she quipped.

Brooke shrugged. "Nah, but I missed sleeping with Wonder Woman. What can I say?" Tess lifted herself off the couch and pulled Brooke to her feet. Brooke kissed her again gently. "I just want to hold you," she said. "One day at a time."

Tess held out her hand and began to lead Brooke up the stairs. *This will not be easy.* Tess giggled.

"Something funny?" Brooke asked as they climbed the stairs.

"No," Tess replied. "No more kissing tonight, though."

"What? Why?"

Tess opened her bedroom door. She turned to Brooke with a sly grin. "Sweetheart," she said affectionately. "I love you. I mean, I really love you." Brooke smiled broadly at the declaration. "I know we are both exhausted," Tess said. Brooke listened. "That kiss of yours could wake the dead," Tess said. "I'm not sure I am quite ready for that yet."

Brooke chuckled. "If I promise to be gentle?" she asked lightly. "Will you at least kiss me goodnight?"

Tess shook her head affectionately. "And here I thought I had to worry about making you angry," she quipped.

It's going to be okay. Brooke kissed Tess on the cheek and headed for the bathroom. Within a few seconds, a hand poked through the door and handed her a familiar pair of sweats.

"Your toothbrush is in the cabinet," Tess said with a snicker.

Brooke laughed when she emerged from the bathroom to find Tess in a similar pair of pajamas. This pair was blue and red with the same Wonder Woman motif. *You are too much.* "Cute," Brooke said.

"I would hate to disappoint you. You said you missed sleeping with Wonder Woman," Tess pointed out as she climbed into the bed.

Brooke slipped under the covers and pulled Tess into her arms. She heard Tess sigh deeply. "I missed sleeping with you," she changed the tenor of their banter. She kissed the top of Tess's head. "I love you, Tess." Tess tightened her hold on Brooke's waist. Brooke felt the slight quivering against her. "Are you okay?"

Tess was giggling. "Yeah, I was just thinking that my mom is going to freak out." Brooke tensed. Tess laughed a bit harder. "She's going to have an inner battle when I bring a beautiful woman home and she just happens to be a doctor."

Brooke snickered. "Go to sleep, Diana."

Tess nestled closer to Brooke with a yawn. "Guess I will be stocking green food a while longer."

Brooke felt Tess's breathing even out and closed her eyes. "One day at a time."

Chapter Nine

Brooke looked down the beach. Her mother was fending off a splash attack from D. and Dani. Brooke rolled her eyes. *She is in her glory.* A voice from above startled her. "Aren't you hot lying out here?" Tess asked. "You look pretty flushed," she commented. She and the kids had been trying to coax Brooke into the water all afternoon. Brooke kept saying she was relaxing.

Brooke loved to swim and to play with the kids, but she was enjoying watching them more. She had no intention of telling any of them that. Her mother had surprised her by booking two small beach houses for a long weekend at Martha's Vineyard. They had arrived late the night before. So late, that by the time everyone had gotten settled, she and Tess had barely made it into bed before falling asleep.

Brooke was also a bundle of nerves. She was pretty sure that Tess knew that. As the weeks passed, the nights she spent at her condo had grown fewer. Most nights, unless she was on call, Brooke slept at Tess's. Slept was the operative word. They had come close a few times to giving in to their desires. It was Brooke who had made the suggestion that, in the interest of one day at a time, they wait to make love. Part of it, and Brooke did not share this with Tess, was that Brooke wanted Tess completely alone the first time they were together. She worried about Davey and Dani. The twins had already accepted Brooke as their mother's girlfriend. That delighted Brooke. The thought of either of the kids walking in when she was making love to their mother unnerved her. She had developed a strange superstition about their first time. Tonight, they would be alone. Brooke was tired of waiting. She intended to make things perfect for Tess. She'd been doing a lot of thinking over the last month, and that led her to some concrete conclusions about where her life was headed.

Tess looked down at Brooke and wanted to laugh. Brooke was a ball of nervous energy. What surprised Tess, was how Brooke was reacting to that. She had become almost introspective in the last twenty-four hours. She suspected that Brooke was watching everything while rolling over the plans she had made in her mind for their evening together. Tess would not have believed it was possible to fall more deeply in love with Brooke than she had been the night Brooke showed up at her door unexpectedly. She had. She was not apprehensive at all about consummating what they had built. She didn't need romantic overtures. She only needed Brooke.

Brooke was looking out at the kids with her mother when she got the shock of a lifetime. "Tess!" Tess was already off running. Brooke stood up, dripping onto her towel. Brooke's scream caused her family to look in her direction and fall into a frenzy of laughter at the sight that greeted them. Brooke's lips upturned into an evil grin and she took off after Tess.

"Now, Brooke," Tess held up a hand when Brooke caught up to her by the water.

"Yes?" Brooke asked while batting her eyelashes. "I know I have warned you about making me angry," Brooke said. In an instant, she had swept Tess into her arms and was moving into deeper water.

"Brooke! Put me down!"

Brooke shrugged. "Okay." She threw Tess into the water. Tess did not surface immediately. "Tess?" In another instant, Brooke was pulled under.

"Where did they go?" Dani asked Brooke's mother.

"Oh, they're fine. I think your mom is teaching Brooke an important lesson."

Brooke broke through a crashing wave and came face to face with a gloating Tess. "Oh…I told you, you wouldn't like me when I'm angry," Brooke said. She moved toward Tess.

Tess took the opportunity to wrap her arms around Brooke's neck. "You don't scare me," Tess laughed.

"What?"

"Nope. You are red. When you turn green, I will run." Brooke huffed and Tess kissed her.

"Ugh," Davey groaned. "They are always doing that."

"I know. So gross," Dani agreed. "Come on, let's find some shells."

Rebecca watched Brooke and Tess and smiled. Brooke's eyes seemed to dance when she looked at Tess. They sparkled in a way that Rebecca had never seen. *I'd get used to it, kids. I have a feeling you are going to be dealing with it for a very long time.*

Tess walked up the small set of stairs to the beach house Rebecca had rented for her and Brooke. The twins were hyper. She had apologized to Rebecca and even offered to have them come back with her. Rebecca laughed and said that if she could survive Brooke for eighteen years, she most certainly could deal with a weekend of Dani and Davey. Tess was grateful for Brooke's mother. Rebecca had not only accepted their relationship, she encouraged it. Rebecca's words as Tess left just minutes ago had taken her by surprise.

"Tess, don't worry. You go and spend some time with Brooke."

"I know they can be a handful."

Rebecca smiled. "You know, I had given up on grandchildren," she said. Tess felt her heart skip. Rebecca chuckled. "Brooke loves you. She loves those kids too. I wish you knew how grateful I am to you."

"To me?" Tess asked. "Why?"

"Because, Tess, Brooke is the most sensitive person I have ever known. She came out of the womb that way, I

swear it." Tess had to chuckle. It was true. Brooke had mastered bravado in front of most of the world. Underneath it, for anyone who cared to take the time to look, Brooke was a mush ball. "She's happy. She finally has what she has always been looking for, it just took her a while to realize that," Rebecca said.

"I hope so," Tess replied.

"I know so," Rebecca assured her with a hug. "Now, get out of here. I will see you tomorrow when I see you."

"I…"

Rebecca laughed heartily. "Contrary to popular opinion, I do have experience with a few things other than surgical techniques." Tess blushed but laughed.

Tess opened the door and lost her breath. The entire room was lit by candles. Brooke stepped into the room wearing a blue sundress. Tess smiled and felt her heart rate increase instantly. *Dear God, she is beautiful.* Brooke smiled nervously and closed the distance between them.

"Hi," she said softly.

"What's the occasion?" Tess asked lightly as she gestured to the room.

"You."

Tess shook her head. "Brooke…"

Brooke took Tess's hand. She started the music system in the small room and turned to Tess. "Would you dance with me?"

Tess smiled and wrapped her arms around Brooke's neck. She didn't recognize the song playing. It was soft and sensual. She would not have been able to concentrate on the words even if she had tried. Brooke's arms were around her. Brooke's hands were softly gliding up and down her back. Tess rested her head against Brooke's chest and listened to the steady thumping of her heartbeat. *I could do this forever.* It was true. Tess desperately wanted to make love with Brooke, but a part of her understood that being in Brooke's arms would always be the safest place on earth.

Brooke lifted Tess's chin and looked into her eyes without words. She captured Tess's lips in a sensuous, kiss. Tess moaned when she felt Brooke's hand press into small of her back. She dropped her hands to Brooke's felt the pace of Brooke's heart increase instantly. Brooke's dropped to Tess's neck, her tongue tasting the flesh beneath it tentatively. "Brooke," Tess sighed.

"I want to give you everything," Brooke whispered in Tess's ear. Tess lost her breath. "I want to make love to you," Brooke said.

Tess looked up at Brooke and cupped her cheek. "Take me to bed."

Brooke nodded. She took hold of Tess's hand and blew out the candles in the room one by one on the way to the small bedroom. When she reached the bedroom, she stopped in the door and looked at Tess apprehensively. Tess pulled her down for a tender kiss of understanding. It did not surprise Tess that their roles were about to reverse. She gently tugged on Brooke's hand and led her to the edge of the bed.

Two months was not an extraordinary amount of time to wait to make love. A month of knowing that you were in love, of sleeping beside one another, of tender caresses, and close calls had built up anticipation in both of them. Tess began placing a trail of delicate kisses down Brooke's throat. Brooke threw her head back against the tender assault. "Tess," she breathed.

Tess smiled to herself and continued to allow her kisses to fall while her hands traversed the silky fabric that covered Brooke's hips. *God, I want you.* Slowly, her hands moved inward over Brooke's stomach and gradually higher. She traced the outline of Brooke's breasts and watched Brooke bite her lower lip. Tess took the cue and allowed the palms of her hands to graze Brooke's already taut nipples. She immediately felt a warm tingle flow through her body and settle in her core. She wanted to explore Brooke's body slowly and thoroughly. That was proving torturous. Tess reached for the straps of Brooke's sundress and lowered them until the dress fell away. She looked at Brooke in wonderment. "You are so beautiful," Tess uttered softly.

Brooke opened her eyes and saw Tess looking at her. Tess's hands were mapping out Brooke's body methodically, every inch of it. When her fingertips reached Brooke's nipples, Tess was helpless not to follow with her lips. She covered one perfect pink peak and tasted it slowly. Brooke's hand moved to the back of Tess's head and held it in place. A deep moan escaped Brooke's lips that urged Tess on. Tess sucked gently and Brooke called out to her.

Brooke reluctantly pulled back. She needed to feel Tess now. Her hands quivered as she reached for the buttons of Tess's white, sleeveless blouse. Tess smiled compassionately at her, passion still lighting her eyes. She took Brooke's hands and steadied them. "It's just me," Tess reminded Brooke.

Brooke leaned in and kissed Tess. "You have no idea what that means," Brooke said.

"Show me," Tess said.

Brooke removed Tess's blouse and caressed the swell of her breasts before reaching back and releasing the clasp of her bra that kept them confined. "Beautiful," she said. She lowered Tess onto the bed and hovered over her. Brooke had taken her share of lovers over the years. She had not once felt anything that compared to what she felt at this moment. It was as if she could feel Tess surrounding her completely. She felt desire, even lust, but something far deeper was driving her now. She needed Tess to understand that Tess was the most important thing in her life. *She is. You are. You are the most important thing in my life.* Brooke was confident in her love for Tess. As she looked down at her soon to be lover, an awareness overtook her that astounded her. If everything else disappeared in her life, her career, her friends, her possessions, it wouldn't matter. All that really mattered were the people she loved. Brooke had never loved anyone the way she loved Tess Sinclair.

Tess watched as a multitude of emotions flickered in Brooke's expression. She was about to speak when Brooke's kiss stopped her. The kiss was more urgent than those that had come before it. It was loving, but insistent as if Brooke needed to say something that she could not find the words to express. Tess's hands moved up and down Brooke's back and continued the motion as Brooke's mouth traveled down her neck to her shoulder and then cautiously inward toward her throat.

"Oh…my… God," Tess panted.

Brooke's lips covered Tess's breast and Tess dug her fingertips into Brooke's back. Brooke had no intention of stopping now. Tess was constantly moaning . Brooke's hands massaged Tess's hips and her thighs. She grabbed hold of the button on Tess's shorts and released it in one deliberate motion. Desire and longing had replaced any apprehension that Brooke had felt when they entered this room. Tess was a part of her, not just her life. She could feel that reality coursing between them. Tess's love was evident in the way her body moved, the way she spoke Brooke's name, it was ever present and never changing. Brooke's kiss moved to Tess's abdomen and she swiftly lowered Tess's shorts and panties together. She stopped and looked at Tess. Tess smiled lovingly. Brooke returned the expression just as Tess took Brooke's hand and kissed her fingertips.

Tess let go of Brooke's hand and Brooke allowed it to travel slowly down Tess's body at the same time her kisses rained downward over Tess's belly. She placed a faint kiss on Tess's center and Tess's hips rose slightly.

Brooke moved still lower and tasted the sweetness that was Tess for the first time.

"Brooke," Tess called helplessly. Brooke's only response response was a lustful moan. Brooke's tongue was swirling around around Tess's center, exploring softly. Tess's hips began to move to move in time with Brooke's gentle licking. She could barely take in a breath against the sensations that were pulsing through her entire body. "Please, please....Brooke," Tess pleaded when Brooke's fingers tenderly brushed over her nipple. Brooke did not need Tess to explain the vague request. She moved her other hand and cautiously entered Tess. "Oh, God!" Tess cried out. Brooke slipped a second finger inside Tess and moved softly deeper. Tess bit her bottom lip hard to keep from screaming. She had never felt anything close to the sensations Brooke was evoking from her body.

Brooke was mesmerized by the way Tess was moving and the subtle changes in her expression. She could feel Tess's muscles gripping her fingers. Brooke moaned. Tess's hips were grinding against her and she was surprised that the twinges of pleasure that she had experienced before had moved to a steady throb. Brooke knew the continual pulsing in her core signaled a brewing storm that would lead to her release. The closer Tess came to letting go, the closer Brooke moved to that same destination. It was so powerful that she was beginning to struggle with concentrating on Tess.

Tess felt Brooke's body beginning to tremble against her. As much as she did not want Brooke to stop what she was doing, she needed to feel Brooke fall over the edge with her. They were both standing on a ledge and Tess wanted to hold Brooke when the freefall began. She wanted Brooke to hold her. She reached down and gently directed Brooke upward.

Brooke's heart dropped for a split second until she saw Tess's seductive smile. Tess kissed Brooke passionately. Her hand took hold of Brooke's hand. Brooke's breath caught in her throat when Tess guided her fingers back to their previous task. Brooke held onto Tess as Tess moved in a circular motion around Brooke's fingers. "You feel so good inside me," Tess told Brooke. "I need to feel you now," she said through a ragged breath.

Brooke sighed when Tess's hand found her and stroked her softness. "Tess," Brooke called. She could not believe that tears were beginning to form in her eyes. She closed her eyes to try and gain control. Her body was succumbing to a wave of indescribable pleasure. She needed to somehow keep her composure.

Tess sensed Brooke's struggle. Brooke's body was moving in harmony with Tess's. The build was slow, like climbing a daunting mountain. One step at a time, their legs grew heavy. It was a pleasurable pain that was stoked by anticipation. At the top, a cliff awaited that hovered over an amazing pool of crystal water. One agonizing, yearning step at a time they traveled upward. Climbing steadily higher, their bodies quivered from exertion. There was no turning back. Tess brushed Brooke's cheek with her other hand. "Open your eyes," she said.

Brooke slowly complied with the request. Her legs were trembling, her heart was racing, and her emotions were overflowing to the point that she feared she might drown in them. Tess smiled softly. "Let go," she said.

Brooke put her forehead against Tess's. "Tess!" she pulled back and called helplessly. Tess held on tightly as Brooke fell first.

Brooke's body began to shake and Tess pulled her back closer as she followed closely behind. "Brooke," Tess called gently. She felt her tears spill over and mix with Brooke's just as Brooke captured her mouth in a passionate kiss. The kiss continued as their bodies moved gradually through the violent jump, into an exhilarating freefall. Wind whipped around them, a rush of pure sensation encompassed them both until they finally reached that serene pool and gently floated home.

"I love you, Tess."

Tess opened her eyes and looked at her lover. "I love you too."

Brooke's heart was still racing. She held Tess close and allowed a comfortable silence to envelop them. She had debated with herself endlessly about what she was about to say. "Tess?"

"Yeah?" Tess answered. She was content lying in Brooke's arms, feeling Brooke against her.

"I want to ask you something," Brooke said.

"You can ask me anything."

"I want you to help me pick out a house," Brooke said in one breath. Tess pulled herself up and looked at Brooke inquisitively. "I'm not asking you to live there... Well, not now anyway," Brooke said. Tess smiled. "If you are seriously married to your house...I mean if you see yourself there forever...I won't look...not that I expect you to want me to move in. But, well, I mean, Murphy needs, and the kids are..."

Tess silenced Brooke with a kiss. She didn't have any doubt about where their relationship was heading. If she had, they would never have traveled to this place. "One day at a time, Brooke. I would love to help you look. If that's what you want."

Brooke's smile warned Tess's heart. "There are a lot of things I want," she said.

"I know," Tess replied. "Me too."

"One day," Brooke said softly.

Tess fell back into Brooke and closed her eyes. *One day, Brooke.* "I love you," Tess whispered.

"I know. I still can't believe it," Brooke confessed. "I landed Wonder Woman."

Tess giggled and smacked Brooke's stomach lightly. "And, I landed a doctor with a green obsession."

"I am not obsessed."

"Go to sleep before you get angry. This bed is need my legroom," Tess said.

Brooke pulled her lover closer. "Goodnight, Diana." Tess was already asleep. "One day, Tess…maybe sooner than you think."

Follow Brooke and Tess on their next adventure in:
SMALL PACKAGES
Available on KINDLE now

Other Series by J.A. Armstrong available on KINDLE
OFF SCREEN
BY DESIGN

Printed in Great Britain
by Amazon

43284760R00076